Joe AND THE
PEACE ETERNAL

Joe AND THE PEACE ETERNAL

JOHN TEOFILO PADILLA JR.

TATE PUBLISHING
AND ENTERPRISES, LLC

Published by Tate Publishing & Enterprises, LLC
127 E. Trade Center Terrace | Mustang, Oklahoma 73064 USA
1.888.361.9473 | www.tatepublishing.com

Tate Publishing is committed to excellence in the publishing industry. The company reflects the philosophy established by the founders, based on Psalm 68:11,
"The Lord gave the word and great was the company of those who published it."

Book design copyright © 2015 by Tate Publishing, LLC. All rights reserved.
Cover design by Joana Quilantang
Interior design by Jake Muelle

Published in the United States of America

ISBN: 978-1-62463-755-1
1. Fiction / Science Fiction / Apocalyptic & Post-Apocalyptic
2. Fiction / Religious
15.11.10

1

"Medical science and the creator!" proclaimed Dr. Robert Benson as he gazed out in reverie through the hospital's staff office window. He feels the warmth of the sunlight strike his skin and the vitamin D synthesis produced endogenously. He stands motionless—leering out through the window at the daily beauty of life. He sees a young boy smiling on his skateboard do two 360-spins effortlessly. He sees an athletic beautiful woman jogging for health. He sees an old man sitting on a bench, feeding pigeons. He sees an old lady, very well dressed, walking her nicely clothed toy poodle in this beautiful city of Beverly Hills. He desires longevity in life for all people while he questions conventional medicine, and marvels at the mysteries of biology that struck others as mundane.

"Thoughts in my mind inform me that monocytes and stem cells can form a symbiosis to cure cancer!" Dr. Benson had said to himself. Suddenly—out of nowhere—a glowing white dove perched on the window ledge next to him. He felt a sudden celestial inner peace and smiled at the beautiful, glowing bright white dove bird. Then he looked up toward the sky, at the fluffy clouds, and proclaimed, "I will find a remedy— for all cancers, mother!"

Meanwhile, a few feet away, Dr. Benson's staff impatiently awaited him.

"Come on, Dr. Benson!" urged his assistant in the staff office. "This is Beverly Hills, in sunny California. Why are you still over there standing like a tree? You're supposed to be in our staff meeting? You think too much? Please come sit and talk with us."

Several new voluptuous female medical interns just sit and leer at him, pondering why the handsome, athletically built Dr. Benson with piercing attractive eyes was somehow not attracted to them.

"Maybe he is not attracted to women," they murmur. "Or maybe he's married without wearing a wedding ring?"

Suddenly, the emergency room's alarm sounds. Dr. Benson and his medical staff quickly scrambled.

"Teamwork!" Dr. Benson shouts. As he entered the emergency room, he observed the ambulance. The emergency medical team had brought in an elderly

Japanese man, so he placed a gentle hand upon him. "I'm the attending physician, Dr. Benson. I will take care of you, Mr. Musashi."

The elderly Japanese man mumbles to the doctor, "Munegaitai. Tasukete!" (My chest hurts. Help me!) Suddenly, Mr. Musashi's eyes ballooned open with fright, as if looking at something paranormal. This worried Dr. Benson.

"Mr. Musashi, please relax!" Dr. Benson tried to soothe him.

But Musashi's frightened eyes stayed open like large watermelons as he said, "Watashi wa karui ishi no shindan o ukete kudasai! Tasukete!" (I see a light, doctor! Help me!) Then his eyes closed.

"Synopsis, nurse!" Dr. Benson requests while he lifts one eyebrow to look directly at Nurse Bianca.

Feeling the burning focus, Nurse Bianca quickly replied, "Dr. Benson, unfortunately Mr. Musashi collapsed from an apparent acute heart attack while in town on a business trip. He was in the process of conducting an informative seminar on living life with peace eternal, when suddenly he experienced tightness in his jaw and chest. Unable to speak, Mr. Musashi then collapsed on the convention floor while giving his presentation."

"Hurry! Time saves muscle!" Dr. Benson commands.

Instantly, an EKG is hooked up to Mr. Musashi, which identifies an acute heart attack. The catheter team quickly inserted a tube into Mr. Musashi's bodily passage and then took pictures, which revealed heart artery blockage. Blood thinners and pain killers are immediately administered to Mr. Musashi while he's taken into the operating room. Dr. Benson scrubs his hands then puts surgical gloves on. *Pop*! The medical team monitors Mr. Musashi's heartbeat while Dr. Benson observes the video camera of the blocked artery. Then Dr. Benson, using a catheter, carefully inserts a stent that looks like a spring of a ballpoint pen into Mr. Musashi. The stent also has a collapsed balloon inside it, which expands as Dr. Benson threads the stent into the lining of Mr. Musashi's blocked artery.

"Heartbeat is steady, doctor," the nurse says. Dr. Benson smiles with confidence then expands the balloon, which expands the stent to scaffold the blocked artery open. Instantly, oxygen rich blood flows to Mr. Musashi's heart.

"I'll insert another stent, which makes two stents," Dr. Benson commands. The medical team continues to monitor Mr. Musashi's good steady heartbeat. Eventually, Dr. Benson authorizes for the patient to be placed into the recovery room. The jubilant medical interns beamed with joy, for Mr. Musashi's life was saved. "Good work team!" Dr. Benson concludes. "Hmm!" Dr. Benson murmurs while he reviews Mr. Musashi's laboratory blood results. "Nurse Bianca, please bring me my special medication disease formula to the recovery room!"

"Yes, doctor, right away!" Nurse Bianca responds. Dr. Benson quickly reviewed his hospital appointment schedule. He quickly observed that an important patient was due to arrive in a half hour. Dr. Benson then stepped into the recovery room to consult his patient Mr. Musashi.

"Watashi wa karui ishi no shindan o ukete kudasai" (Thank you for saving my life doctor,) Mr. Musashi said as Dr. Benson entered the recovery room.

"If you're thanking me, please wait, Mr. Musashi. Unfortunately, you have other health issues that need to be addressed!" Mr. Musashi was ethically informed of his Parkinson's, Alzheimer's, and arthritis. "The good news, Mr. Musashi, is that I have been working on a remedy for all these health concerns. And with your permission, I could administer my special new medicine. However, I would need for you to be available for follow-up medical appointments?"

"Ossu," Mr. Musashi replied.

"Hai! Yes that's right! My Japanese is very rusty. I haven't practiced it since I was a child, but I know a little from my father's military tour there. Please speak to me in English, Mr. Musashi." The old man nodded yes, so he continued. "Good then, since we now have an understanding, I project you living many more years." At that moment, the lovely, well-educated Nurse Bianca brought in the new medicine, which biologist Dr. Benson created himself in the laboratory. Nurse Bianca enjoys being next to Dr. Benson for many reasons; however, she does not enjoy witnessing the administration of the new medicine prototype.

"Here is the new medicine, and I've brought the consent form, Dr. Benson," Nurse Bianca says.

"Yes. Thank you, Ms. Bianca." Dr. Benson handed the consent forms to Mr. Musashi, and he signs them to receive the new medication. Then Nurse Bianca departs to place it in records. After a short pause, Dr. Benson goes over Mr. Musashi's blood laboratory results. Mr. Musashi attempts to read Dr. Bensons mind by looking into the spirit of his eyes, which some say are the windows to a humans' soul.

Dr. Benson feels this, so he breaks the staring game, and says, "Mr. Musashi, I understand that you give seminars on peace eternal?"

"Hai. Yes. I mean yes, doctor," Mr. Musashi says.

"What is peace eternal?" Dr. Benson asked.

"Find your gift inside you," Mr. Musashi proclaims. "However, this alone does not give you peace eternal. Peace eternal takes time to explain. It involves a personal journey a person takes in life. In my seminar, I explain thoroughly the inner self and a journey a person takes along the way to achieve peace eternal."

"Does poor health harm or interfere with peace eternal?"

"Yes, Dr. Benson. Poor health interferes some with peace eternal." Mr. Musashi says. "A person needs to be pure in good thought, and not worry. You see, if a person worries, or is ill and worries about their illness, then this distracts them from achieving their goal."

And Dr. Benson says, "Do you have family or children?"

"Yes." Mr. Musashi looks at Dr. Benson firmly. "Do you, Dr. Benson, also have children?"

"No, I do not have children yet. However, poor health and your peace eternal as you say. We need to address, Mr. Musashi." Dr. Benson reaffirms.

"Dr. Benson, have you found peace and your gift inside yourself yet?" Mr. Musashi investigates.

"No, I have not found my peace, but I've found my quest. I'm searching for the cure to remedy all cancers in humans," Dr. Benson says with a determined face.

"Good. You are on your personal journey?"

"Yes, it's a hard personal journey. When I'm not working in the hospital, I'm in the laboratory all night long."

A nurse suddenly brings a cup of coffee inside the recovery room, and she hands it to Dr. Benson.

"Thank you, nurse." Dr. Benson says as the nurse quickly departs the scene. "Mmm. Now that's one good cup of joe!"

"Again, I am very grateful, doctor," Mr. Musashi states.

As Dr. Benson listens, he reflects on the day, drinking his coffee. "I am very grateful, too, Mr. Musashi. It's an honor for me to help all humans."

Mr. Musashi pauses for energy, then focuses completely in the direction of Dr. Benson. "One day I will honor my gratitude by giving you honor," Mr. Musashi proclaims.

"Ossu?" Dr. Benson says. "But for now, Mr. Musashi, I'm ready to administer my new medication, so prepare yourself and get ready, sir." Consciously, Mr. Musashi prepares himself as he took in a few deep breaths of air, then he closed his eyes for meditation. After a brief moment, as he slowly opened up his eyes, they frightfully ballooned up open like large watermelons again. He observed Dr. Benson holding a huge, thick needle. Dr. Benson slowly squirted out some medicine and he got out some air bubbles.

Dr. Benson said, "Relax, Mr. Musashi! This won't hurt me, so it shouldn't hurt you...." Then Mr. Musashi slowly felt the huge, cold needle inserted into his thick shoulder muscle. "Please don't worry, Mr. Musashi. I'm a biologist. I really, truly need this special big needle, to insert the large dose of my thick, special medication." Dr. Benson says with a comforting voice. Nevertheless, Mr. Musashi feels the thick medicine trickling into his veins, so he moans a little. Upon administering medication, he monitored Mr. Musashi for a few minutes, then he exited the recovery room.

"Nurse Bianca, please continue to monitor Mr. Musashi. I have to go see a scheduled appointment," Dr. Benson instructed then he departed the area. As he walked, he sipped on his cup of coffee. Suddenly, his cell phone rings. It's his father, General Benson. "Yes, father?"

"Son, Robert, my mission is about wrapped up, so I'm going to come and visit you for a while." General Benson says as he scans the perimeter through his huge binoculars, witnessing his soldiers in hand-to-hand combat against the enemy element.

"Yes, father. Please let yourself in when you arrive if I'm not home. I still have a mission of my own!"

"Yes, I know, son. I miss your mother, but we still have each other, son. I love you, and I'll see you soon, Robert."

"Be careful, father. See you soon." Dr. Benson says. Then he takes an elevator to go upstairs several floors away from the operating and recovery rooms. Upon arriving, he gulps down the last few drops of his quality coffee. Thinking of osteopathy, Dr. Benson looked forward to treating his scheduled patient. As he exits the elevator, he does a few basketball shuffle steps then dunks his empty coffee cup into a nearby trash can. Dr. Benson, with proud medical confidence, smoothly entered the room to see his scheduled patient named Adolfo, whom is an aging male ballet dancer.

Adolfo willingly receives medical treatment from the young but brilliant physician and biologist Robert Benson. Dr. Benson's main concern is to cure all cancers and to keep humans living as long as medically possible. He does not violate the Controlled Substance Act of 1970, and he is registered as a health professional with the Drug Enforcement Agency. Dr. Benson does have ethics based on the Blanchard and Peale model. However, he does use medicine with an unbeknown secret substance using imagination and diligent concentration. Dr. Benson has created new and effective medicines. Unfortunately, only the rich and famous know about his medical wizardry. A malpractice lawsuit does not worry Dr. Benson, and he has yet been subject to any lawsuits of any kind. As Dr. Benson says, "Res ipsa locuitur" (The thing speaks for itself).

—〰—

In a far-off distant country, there are the sounds of heavy gunfire. A war is in progress while General Benson takes out of his pocket a cigarette rolling paper. Then he places it in his left palm, between the crease of his thumb and middle finger. A little on edge, he grabs a small pouch of tobacco and sprinkles it into the paper. He uses his fingers and thumbs to quickly roll the paper firmly, keeping the tobacco inside. He licks the edges of the paper horizontally left to right and seals the tightly rolled cigarette. Then he puts the smooth-tasting cigarette in his mouth as he pulls out a wooden matchstick from his tanned Stetson hat. Needing a hard surface, he strikes the match on the steel helmet of Captain Malarkey, who is next to him.

Fire is created, and General Benson brings the match's fire slowly to the edge of his cigarette.

"Puff, puff. Mmm!" General Benson says to calm his nerves. General Benson looks through his wide-lens binoculars downrange. He sees a muscular army ranger stealthily moving through enemy territory. General Benson loses vision of the army ranger as he disappears like a ghost. At that moment, he sees a civilian with a camera around his neck, unnoticed by the enemy—dipping and darting around like a jackrabbit—slithering children out of enemy territory. General Benson continues to hold his binoculars with his left hand, and he twirls his right pointing finger in a small circle around his right temple.

"Das ist kaputt (You are crazy)!" General Benson says. "Captain Malarkey! Who is that yahoo down there?"

Captain Malarkey zooms in using his own binoculars, and says, "That's Angelo, civilian news photographer."

General Benson, with American pride, says, "Wow! Angelo just saved a large group of children hiding in a ground hole. I wish he was one of my soldiers." Suddenly, there's a loud boom in the area were Ranger Bill disappeared, followed by heat smoke in the air. As it appears, the dangerous enemy element, which caused General Benson so much havoc, is no more! General

Benson scans the area with his binoculars but he sees no movement.

"Not even a mouse stirring down there, but…" General Benson whispers as he lowers his binoculars to hang from the strap around his neck. "It's quiet down there, captain, but I feel uneasy."

"Yeah, me too!" Captain Malarkey says. "But it appears Ranger Bill took out the element almost single-handedly." General Benson raised his binoculars and got on the radio—breaking the silence. "Kremlin to tiger, what's your 10-20?"

Ranger Bill's rustic voice comes over the radio, "Higher! Tiger to Kremlin. Mission 10-4!"

General Benson beams with pride as he lowers his binoculars to hang by the strap around his neck. "Now, I feel easy and safe."

But Captain Malarkey says, "General, sir, I worry about your safety, wearing that big old Stetson hat! It's not a helmet sir, and when shrapnel flies, doggies cry!"

General Benson looks Captain Malarkey straight in the eyes. "Dummkopf (Idiot)! I wear this big cowboy hat to keep the sunlight and moonlight out of my eyes. My increased vision keeps my soldiers safer, and I feel more in control of winning!" Captain Malarkey is at a loss for words, so he just nods his head in approval.

—⁕—

In appreciation for Dr. Benson's medical help, Adolfo offers him tickets to the next English Ballet Theatre show. Dr. Benson smiles and thanks him, but says he is very busy and probably will not have time to attend.

"Young man," Adolfo says, "it's good to have goals in life, but a person should fill their time with all the good, fun memories life can offer. Just remember, the end of days is approaching, and there's no guarantee that there will be a tomorrow. Tomorrow may never come!"

Dr. Benson ponders Adolfo's advice. "Wise words, Adolfo, but there's currently nothing inspiring me to have more fun in life. I appreciate your thoughtfulness, but I am content with my life as it is now." He then informs Adolfo that he probably won't be able to walk very well for a few days, but with Dr. Benson's special medicine, he should recover well enough to do a few more years of ballet.

Adolfo, who learned of the great Dr. Benson in confidence from a celebrity entertainer, doesn't know what's in the medicine other than natural herbs. Dr. Benson explains that his medicine is a combination of extracts from various plants, minerals, natural spring water, oxygen drawn from healthy ocean air, and insect enzymes. This special blend is somehow designed to work with human DNA. Dr. Benson believes his medicine can provide a foundation for cures and preventative compounds for cancers, AIDS, and other diseases. Adolfo, though, just wants to be able to perform again.

"I have other patients to help now, but I'm worried about how you'll get home since you can't walk," Dr. Benson says. "A nurse can get you one of the hospital wheelchairs, and I will be glad to call a cab for you, but once you reach your house—"

"My daughter is coming to pick me up," Adolfo assures him. "Dr. Benson, young man, you should see the beauty of the ballet. It will inspire you and bring enthusiasm to your life."

A few seconds pass, Dr. Benson replies, "I wish I had the time, Adolfo."

Just then, Adolfo's daughter walked into the room, gliding gracefully with each step. It was as if a beautiful flower or angel had just arrived. Young Dr. Benson's eyes light up; he hears music in his soul.

"What is her name?" Dr. Benson asks quietly.

"I know she warms your heart, young man," says the old dancer. "My daughter's name is Olivia, and she is the best ballerina any theater will ever have. She is what she is! An angel. She shows how very beautiful life can be."

Olivia smiles. "Thank you immensely, Dr. Benson. May I please wheel my father out of the hospital?"

"The rules of the hospital state that only medical staff can escort patients outside," the doctor explains. "But Adolfo is my patient, and somehow I cannot say no to you, Ms. Olivia. Yes, you may escort your father to your car. But Adolfo, doctor's orders, do not get out of the wheelchair! Let your daughter push you."

As Olivia takes hold of the wheelchair, Adolfo presses the ballet tickets into Dr. Benson's hand. "Thank you, Adolfo," says Dr. Benson. "And you may keep the wheelchair."

Olivia's eyes connect with Dr. Benson's, and she smiles in gratitude. She waves as they leave the office. Dr. Benson watches until she is out of view. He can't stop thinking how Olivia looks like a most beautiful flower—or how her aroma was like the most wonderful perfume he'd ever smelled.

After meeting Olivia, Dr. Robert Benson's mind, heart, body, and soul could not focus on anything but getting to the ballet to have a chance at seeing her again. He felt something stir in his chemistry—something awoke inside him. He convinced a few of his colleagues to treat themselves to some leisure time and join him for the ballet, but in reality he knew he was just trying to find an excuse to attend himself.

—⚬—

The ballet opened with an orchestra playing harmonious classical music that calmed the soul. Olivia, as the star of the English Ballet Theatre, had requested it, and she got anything she asked. The show's director and producer required only that the ballet show must go on, but the rest was up to her. This particular performance had been choreographed by Adolfo and Olivia themselves. As the music began, a huge array of beautiful flowers was placed on stage, allowing the audience to enjoy its wonderful scent while listening to peaceful celestial music.

A spotlight came on and lit up center stage; it focused on Olivia, illuminating her beautiful face and body. In Dr. Benson's eyes, she looked just like an angel. She started to spin gracefully with the music, enchanting the audience as she glided across the floor. The music changed pleasantly then more dancers entered the stage and formed a human wall. Suddenly, Olivia leapt high in the air, over the other performers. It seemed like she could stay in the air forever. The audience gasped in awe at her extraordinary athletic ability. Olivia landed softly *sur la pointe*—one leg in the air—her arms open as if to hug the audience with her voluptuous body. Her gorgeous eyes sparkled, making the audience swoon in their desire to hug her back.

The music changed again, and Olivia began to dance to a harp solo, charming the spirit of the audience to sweat beads of perspiration while they watched her extraordinary performance. The harpist was a great musician called Jubal, just like the musician in the Holy Bible. Olivia suddenly leapt what seemed to be about twenty feet high in the air, and as she started to glide down to earth, a hand emerged out of nowhere to catch her. It was her father, Adolfo. He held her high above his head, and the people started to cry with joy and clapped till their hands hurt. The full symphony swelled as all of its musical instruments sung in a harmony so pleasing to the ear that the audience began to hug one another as if they were brothers and sisters.

The lights dimmed, and the music faded away. The show was over. Dr. Benson lingered in his seat, reluctant to see the evening come to an end. Suddenly, a soft hand touched his shoulder.

"Thank you again, Doctor, for curing my father," Olivia says. "Without him, the show would not exist."

Adolfo overhears his daughter's words and laughs. "No, no, Olivia! They all come to see you. You know that I am also one of your biggest fans, my beautiful daughter."

Dr. Benson's testosterone begins to surge through his veins as he looks at Olivia, and he says, "May I invite the both of you for a cup of joe?"

"A cup of joe?" Olivia asks.

"It is honor enough to be invited, Dr. Benson, but my old bones must go home and rest," Adolfo says. "However, you have my permission to ask my daughter."

Dr. Benson considers the ethics of the situation. Adolfo is his patient—is it wise or proper for Dr. Benson to date his daughter? But he is overwhelmed by Olivia. It is as if he is in the presence of an angel from God. He lets his eyes meet hers as he considers what to say. But before he can say anything, she smiles at him and says, "Yes, I would love to, Dr. Benson." They continue to smile at each other and say good-bye to Adolfo.

Dr. Benson interlocked his arm gently with Olivia's and escorted her to a small café nearby. He opened the door affectionately, allowing her to walk in first. He held her chair out while she sat, like a gentleman.

"Two cups of joe, please!" he calls to the waitress.

They drink their coffee companionably.

"What do you have in your suit pocket, Dr. Benson?" Olivia asks.

He laughs. "You have enhanced observation skills. Is it because you're an entertainer? And please, call me Robert."

"All right then, Robert. What is it I see in your suit pocket?"

"It's a book I am currently reading. I always carry a book with me."

"May I see it?"

He hands it to her. She is astonished. "*Plants of the World*. I love botany too!" They look at the book together and find themselves holding hands, sipping their coffee, and sitting like two lovebirds who just enjoy being close to each other.

The waitress comes over and says, "Another cup of joe for the gentleman and lady?"

They looked into each other's eyes. Both want to continue their enjoyable companionship. They say at the same time, "Yes, please!"

"Robert, why is coffee called a cup of joe?" Olivia asks.

"It's military slang. My father, Arnold, taught me the phrase. He's still in the military. It was my mother's favorite slang term. She would use it to get us all laughing."

"Your mother sounds like a fine, charismatic lady." A sad look came over his face. "I'm sorry, Robert," Olivia says. "Did she pass away?"

It emerges that both of their mothers died from cancer. Dr. Benson explains that this loss prompted him to become a biologist as well as a medical doctor, and that his chief goal is finding a cure for cancer. Olivia says that she has already achieved her first life's goal—mastering ballet and becoming a successful ballerina. Her next goal, she says, is to tend a splendid garden and to create a beautiful family.

They continued to enjoy their coffee and each other's company for hours.

At the end of the night, Dr. Benson blurted out, "Olivia, may I please see you again?"

Her face shone with happiness. She looked deep into his eyes and said, "It would be an honor and pleasure to see you again, Robert."

2

D r. Benson lamented to himself that a day that lasted only twenty-four hours was not long enough—not long enough to allow him to find a cure for cancer, anyway.

"I must find a cure for cancer! I will find a cure for cancer!" he shouted.

To find subjects for his unconventional trials, he had resorted to adopting cats and dogs from various animal shelters. He particularly liked adopting animals that were sick, believing it was more humane to attempt to cure a sick animal than to allow the shelter to kill it. He also looked in the newspapers for offers to adopt free animals, like when owners could not take care of their pets any longer for various reasons. Some of the animals had cancerous skin growths, which pleased him. He hoped his humane experiments might cure them.

Dr. Benson worked many hours alone, and sometimes talked aloud to himself. "I know I'm not supposed to experiment on humans the way I do on animals," he mused. "But how will I know if my cures work on people?" There was not a second, minute, or hour that Dr. Benson did not concentrate on his burning desire to cure cancer. He remembered his mother's last moments, when he cried with her and promised he would find a cure.

One day, an amazing thing happened. Dr. Benson received a package labeled Hopefully from a rich old man named John Hughes, a patient of his. Inside he found unidentified materials, and a well-kept secret manuscript of Sir Isaac Newton, a brilliant scientist and alchemist who is well-known for believing he had deciphered a code in the Holy Bible. He had calculated that the world would end in 2060. The package has a letter from Mr. John Hughes.

> Dr. Benson,
>
> Sir, this package was recovered by my lead investigator from a monk at an unidentified monastery in an isolated region of the world. The monk was tactfully interrogated by my investigator, and true or false, this was the information retrieved from the now, unfortunately deceased monk!

Recorded by Monk Fritz is the following:

> Isaac Newton's last days—saw God as the masterful creator whose existence could not be denied in the face of the grandeur of all creation. Newton had searched, his colleagues later confessed to me—for the scientific evidence that God existed. Apparently, or perhaps, he had discovered it. Unfortunately, before Newton went public, Jesuit Samhain discovered Sir Isaac Newton dead in his laboratory. The Jesuit also discovered recent manuscripts burned to ashes in Newton's fireplace—close to his dead body. Later, it is the authorities who took hair samples of Sir Isaac Newton for an autopsy, which revealed Newton expired from a combination of arsenic and mercury poisoning. In conclusion, Jesuit Samhain believed Newton died of self-inflicted wounds.

"Hmm! I wonder?" Dr. Benson says. Fortunately for mankind, Dr. Benson, a brilliant biologist and bio-chemist, will stop at nothing to find a cure for cancer. He systematically searched the package for clues. "Yes! This could be possibly my missing link!" He reflected on Newton's life while he read methodically through Newton's manuscript, wondering if they mentioned any plants that Newton used through innovative ways. Yet, the sleepless and tired Dr. Benson had only found in this package mathematical formulas of various metal experiments, which included arsenic and mercury, along with personal religious materials. "I will send these mathematical formulas to a newly formed company called Saman Industries! Maybe they can decipher the unusual mathematical formulas?"

Like Newton, Dr. Benson believed there might be a connection between God and science. Since God created the world, Dr. Benson reasons, he could also use science to manipulate the world—creating earthquakes, floods, tsunamis, and volcanic eruptions, for example. Dr. Benson believed such events were one way God cleanses the world and lets you know he exists.

At nine the following Saturday morning, Dr. Benson was getting ready to leave his home on the outskirts of Beverly Hills to begin making house calls. He gets into his Mercedes-Benz SLS AMG supercar and fires up the ignition.

"I love the way this engine sounds," he says to himself. He plays his favorite music on the car's stereo and makes his way to the estate of John Hughes nearby. Mr. Hughes's cancer had gone into remission thanks to Dr. Benson's latest medication and subconscious mind therapy. Today, Benson will administer Mr. Hughes's medicine and give him a physical treatment.

Dr. Benson drove up the private road cautiously to the mansion and arrived by quarter to ten at the security check point. A large man with darkly shaded glasses and a suit motion for Dr. Benson to get out of his vehicle. Dr. Benson complied with instructions and raised his hands—extended them horizontally—as armed security guards gave him a clothed pat down to be checked for weapons, then with an electronic wand to be check for concealed weapons. Mr. Hughes is overcautious and anxious to live an extremely long life, thus this was routine. Dr. Benson was cleared to proceed ahead to meet with his patient.

The medical evaluation finally begins with Dr. Benson palpating his patient's lymph nodes to check for any deformities.

"Let me see you smile, John," he says. "Don't forget the subconscious constructive mind therapy."

"Yes, Dr. Benson, I know! I keep repeating to myself, 'I feel great! I have no cancer! I am cured!'" Then he asked the question Dr. Benson feared was coming. "Are you close to finding a cure for cancer yet?"

"Yes, I am close. I have discovered how to extend the life of animals with cancer, just as I have for humans, but they still die eventually. I believe a plant extract that has not yet been discovered will help, possibly from a species that lives in an extreme location, like in the crater of a volcano or in the deep ocean."

"Look inside my greenhouse at the plants my scientific and archeological teams just brought in," Mr. Hughes says. "If you do not find what you need, rest assured that I will send them on another expedition."

Dr. Benson visits the greenhouse but does not find anything he has not used before. He returns to Mr. Hughes and asks, "When is your next shipment of plants coming in? And when I come next time, may I bring a lady friend?"

"Sure, young man, bring your girlfriend. There should be a new shipment of plants coming soon."

Thinking hard, Dr. Benson quietly said good-bye. Since his large brain drifted into intuitive thought processes, he did not see the evil smile that flickered across Mr. Hughes's face as he pulled out a cigar, bit off the end, put it in his mouth, and lit it. He puffed away, and a cloud of smoke surrounded him as he snickered.

———✕———

In the back yard of her father's home, Olivia had set up a customized ballet exercise gym. Every morning,

Olivia began her rigorous training regimen of flexibility, core strength, feet strengthening, leaping, balance, and mind-stage control. She started her regimen with flexibility. She would lie down on the gym mat floor to find a comfortable spot while she opened her legs in a splits position.

"Yes. That's good." Olivia says. She then placed one foot forward and the other foot to the rear as she switched feet to get an even stretch. She moved on to powerful core Pilates exercises. This was to maintain her powerful ballerina abdominals essential for her pointe preparation.

"Replenish time!" Olivia says. She eats a piece of fruit, drinks some water, and wipes her face with her towel that's by her workout station. She takes a few relaxing energy breaths and goes into foot strengthening. She moved into the first position and faced the barre. Then she rolled up adagio—or slowly on the ball of her toes to full pointe—rolled down to three-quarter pointe, and pressed back up to pointe. She rolled down to flat, demi-plie in first, and straightened her legs. She took a break then went into her balance regimen as she stood on one foot for half an hour then switched to the other foot to do the same. She would also use one foot at a time to stand on her front toes for good period of time. She took a break to drink some water that she has close by. Now, she prepares mentally for mind stage control. She turned on her backyard noise and music system. It had a combination of abusive gestures, fans jeering and clapping, but on the other side music. She put the music lower then the people's noise as she smiled in front of a large mirror doing ballerina moves. Olivia smiled with joy because her favorite time is the leaping regimen. Olivia ran fast then did a brisé, or jump onto the trampoline. As she rocketed upward with each jump using her mind attempting to touch the clouds, she got higher and higher. Adolfo happened to walk by the family room adjacent to the backyard. He observed Olivia springing high on the trampoline, fluttering her legs.

He cried with pride, "That's my little girl!"

3

Though Dr. Benson was extremely busy, he talked to Olivia on the phone whenever he could. If several days passed by without seeing her, it felt to him as if it had been weeks. But then an exciting day came—his beautiful ballerina was returning after a tour, and he was going to John Hughes's greenhouse to inspect various plants that had just arrived. It was a warm Sunday, and Dr. Benson started his ocean-blue Mercedes and put in a Beatles CD. He took off so fast he burned rubber, but he didn't care; he had the money to buy new tires. He flew down straight roads, singing along to "Let It Be," and slowing just enough to take turns safely.

He allowed his mind to drift back into the past as he remembered being eleven years old again. He remembered being with his mother and father on the German autobahn inside a comfortable car that moved fast. His father, Arnold, was stationed in Germany then, and his mother, Mary, was a native German. His dad would get his hands on various German cars for the weekends so they could travel different, challenging autobahns and explore different German cities. Sometimes his dad would drive, and sometimes his mom would. At some point, she would always say, out of the blue, "Cup of joe!" They would get off the autobahn and find some coffee. Dr. Benson liked drinking coffee even as a child, but his mother would make him drink delicious German hot chocolate instead if it was late in the day so he wouldn't be up all night. They were great times.

Dr. Benson's mind flashed back to when his mother got sick with breast cancer and was bedridden in the hospital. His grandfather, Dr. Hans, was a good German physician but he was unable to cure his only daughter.

When she was near death, he kissed her forehead and said tearfully, "Good-bye, Mary! I will always love you!" Then he left little Robert and his father alone to say good-bye.

Tears rolled down Robert's face as he said, "I will be the best doctor in the world, Mommy, just like Grandfather Hans, and I will cure people from cancer. And then I'll be able to cure you too. Please don't leave us, Mommy!"

"Your grandfather will always be with you in spirit to help you, my beautiful son," she said. "I, too, will always be with you whenever you think of me. My little Robert, how I love you! Mommy is with you always." Then she smiled at her son and died in her husband's arms.

They cried together over her loss, deep in sorrow. Robert kissed his mother and said, "I will always think of you, Mommy."

After that, Arnold Benson buried himself in his military career; getting promoted to higher ranks became his only goal. He sent his son to the best schools to study medicine and biology. No matter where they were stationed, they found Robert the best education. Dr. Benson greatly appreciated his father's sacrifice, and he devoted himself to his studies. He never wavered from his goal of finding a cure for cancer.

Dr. Benson shifted the Mercedes into high gear as he sped over to Olivia's house. It was afternoon by the time he arrived. He saw her watching him from the window as he got out of the car, wearing his English summer sports coat. Olivia's eyes made instant contact with him for a pleasant moment. He went up to the front door and rang the doorbell—only once—he's a gentleman and knew that ceaseless buzzing could be annoying.

Olivia opened the door. "Robert! I have been expecting you, please come in." He handed her a bouquet of flowers, kissed her hand, and looked into her eyes. At that moment, there was no need for him to tell her that she was beautiful. She knew how he felt. He liked her and wanted to be with her.

Olivia, a fine and proper young lady, felt the chemistry between them. Dr. Benson stepped inside. He knew from their first-date conversation that she enjoyed flowers and plants like he did.

"Ms. Olivia," he says, "I would be honored if you would accompany me to view an exhibit of rare and exotic plants and flowers."

"I would be honored, Robert, and I would love to. But first, will you speak to my father?" She escorted him to the living room where Adolfo sat waiting.

"Please sit down, Dr. Benson," he says.

Dr. Benson sat down on one of the room's fine European chairs.

"May I bring something for you two gentlemen to drink?" Olivia asked. "Perhaps lemonade, coffee, tea, or something a little stronger?" She is such a lady and thoughtful hostess.

"How about a cup of joe?" Dr. Benson asks.

Adolfo laughs. "I'll have a cup of coffee, too, please, sweetheart."

Several minutes later, Olivia brought them the coffee in fine china cups. "I will leave you two gentlemen alone to talk for a few moments."

As she walked away, Dr. Benson watched a vision of grace disappear from sight. When she was out of earshot, Adolfo said, "I have been getting a lot of migraine headaches. How are my blood and urine lab results?"

Dr. Benson wanted to be sensitive to his patient's feelings, but medical ethics obligated him to inform Adolfo of the truth. "Well, sir, the good news is that for the most part, your muscles and organs are like those of a healthy twenty-year-old, and the medication I gave you has rejuvenated your mobility. However, I'm afraid that your lab results show cancer in your blood. I'm sorry, Adolfo. I do have a medication that's not yet approved for consumer use, but it could extend your life a little more. I could administer this medication with your permission, though it goes against ethical practices. I take this step when I want to buy more time for my patients and their loved ones. It's your decision, but I recommend it. My cancer patients have had longer lives after taking this medication. It slows the cancer down. I know that this is stopping short of success. It is only a temporary remedy. I will not rest until I find a complete cure for all cancers."

"Hmm," Adolfo says. "Dr. Benson, what do you think about my daughter, Olivia?"

He paused, deep in thought. "Sir, I know this may be sudden, but…I respectfully ask your permission to marry her. I love her!"

"You have my permission, young man. It would be an honor to have such an intelligent doctor in our family. But of course, it is my daughter's decision in the end, and I will respect it!"

"Yes, I understand."

"I have made up my mind, Dr. Benson! Please administer your new cancer medicine. I have many good reasons to live longer, my boy! I know you will find a cure for cancer eventually. Also, Doctor, I request your solemn oath as a physician that you will not tell my daughter about my cancer."

"You have my word, sir." They shook hands, then Olivia returned. Dr. Benson felt like she lit up the entire room.

"I'm ready when you are," she says.

"You young people go out and have fun," Adolfo says. "Please don't rush back. I have a good book to read, and maybe I'll have a nice quiet nap."

"Enjoy your day, Father."

"Don't worry, Mr. Adolfo. I will keep Olivia safe, you have my word. About everything." They exchanged smiles.

Dr. Benson and Olivia departed.

Dr. Benson's Mercedes roared on the secluded open highway. Olivia was holding on to her passenger's seat, but she seemed to be enjoying the ride. She caught Robert's eye occasionally, and the rest of the time kept an eye on the road.

"I like the sound of a finely tuned automobile," he says as he puts some celestial music on low.

"Mmm. Notice how the music notes blend, Robert."

He looked at her, admiring her not only for her beauty but also for her musical knowledge. "Do you play any instruments, Olivia?"

"Yes, my father and mother required me to learn piano when I was a little girl. They said it would be part of my social development and help make me a better person."

Dr. Benson's heart swelled. "I enjoy listening to good classical music. It would make my entire week if I could hear you play piano sometime."

"Of course." She smiled, showing her perfectly straight teeth. "Music helps me enormously, especially when I dance. I am able to put my heart into the ballet because I know the music, and I can leap and spin better for understanding the meaning behind the notes A through G. Music has history, theory, technique, and performance. The bass clef means low sounds. The treble clef means high sounds. Music learned at a young age opens the mind for higher education, and instills peace in your character to resolve obstacles in your life."

"I am very impressed with the way you think."

They arrived at John Hughes's estate. The entrance gate has a camera and an external speaker box. A voice came through it. "Come on in, Dr. Benson. We have been expecting you." The gate opened, and they pulled up to the security checkpoint, where they were asked to exit the vehicle.

"Don't worry, Olivia, this is just routine," Dr. Benson says. "The security personnel will inspect us for weapons."

She took his hand. "When I am with you, Robert, I feel safe."

A female security guard inspected Olivia, and a male security guard inspected Dr. Benson while a separate team of guards inspected the Mercedes. Upon completion of the inspections, one of the guards looked at Olivia, who was standing next to the car.

"Wow!" he says. "Now that's beautiful!"

The rest of the security guards look down, wishing they weren't there. Dr. Benson glared at the guard.

He was sure the man was talking about Olivia and not the car.

"If you have honor, sir, it would behoove you to apologize," Dr. Benson says, though he feels like slamming the cad on the car and breaking some of his bones. He is a physician, after all, so his knowledge of anatomy allowed him to picture exactly which ones would crack.

"I'm very sorry, please forgive me, both of you," the security guard says.

"I would like to see my patient now, please," Dr. Benson says as he escorts Olivia away from the ignorant individual. He knew he could control himself but he also knew he could not control other people.

His usual tactic was to avoid confrontation if possible. People who weren't content with their lives were unpredictable, and besides, he didn't want to waste his precious time on them. Dr. Benson escorted Olivia to the huge greenhouse. John Hughes was waiting there.

"Robert, look," Olivia says as she took in all the beautiful flowers, many of which she had never seen before.

They walked around together through the rare, exotic plants. Dr. Benson explained the information cards sitting next to each flower. "These tell us where the plant was discovered and the scientific name the plant was given." Dr. Benson said.

Olivia picked up a card from beside a flower she liked. "Robert, this says the plant was discovered thousands of feet below sea level in the rain forest. There was an earthquake that formed a crack in the earth. There lay the sole plant deep by a natural water well, which cost many lives that attempted to retrieve the plant, for Mr. Hughes. Incredible!" Olivia says and ponders. "Robert, why would someone go to such lengths and possible danger to find such a plant?"

Suddenly, the rich and old Mr. Hughes walked up to them, seemingly from out of nowhere. "I can answer that question, young lady. And the plant you were looking at, my scientist believe it came from the ancient time of Noah, from the rings of markings in the earth below, where the plant was discovered. Listen, I am old and have more money than I'll ever need, and sadly my wife is no longer alive to travel with me." A sad expression came over his face. "I now have expert travelers who go places for me. I want to stay close to home to watch my grandkids grow up. I'm also a patient of Dr. Benson's. With your permission, I respectfully request a few moments alone with my doctor. There is freshly squeezed fruit juice on the table, please help yourself."

"I am thirsty," Olivia says. "Please, Robert, help your patient. He seems to be a nice, courteous gentleman. I will be back shortly."

"I will be close by you always!" Dr. Benson says. Olivia walked away to pour herself some juice, but she was still within his sight line.

"I'm sorry for what happened earlier, regarding my security man's comments. I assure you, he no longer exists!" Mr. Hughes said.

Dr. Benson knows he cannot control the rich man's actions, but he trembles to think that Mr. Hughes might have just had the guard killed on his account. Instead, he concentrated on the vast variety of plants, smelling them and feeling them with his fingers. *Perhaps one of them contained the enzyme I needed to cure cancer*, he thought.

Just then, another man walked into the room. Dr. Benson noticed that he wore the same ring as John Hughes. He believed it was a Water Mason ring. He looked wealthy too. He nodded a greeting to Dr. Benson and said, "Mr. Hughes, a word, please?"

Mr. Hughes stepped away. A few moments passed as Dr. Benson studied some plants. Suddenly, Olivia came back with her soft stealth feet; her hand warmly touched his arm.

"Robert, can I have this plant?" she asks.

He looked at the plant she was pointing to. It was a beautiful flower with exotic colors that seemed to change when light or shade fell over it.

"Interesting plant," he says. "You sure have good eyes." While she wasn't looking, he slipped a small envelope under the flower.

"The plant is yours," he said. "But look! That envelope has your name on it."

Olivia looked deep into his eyes, as if attempting to read his thoughts. Then she picked up the envelope. She opened it and took the note from inside. She read it aloud, softly.

"I love you, Olivia. Please marry me! Robert." Tears ran down her face. She smiled and locked eyes with him again, looking more like an angel than ever. "Yes, Robert," she says. "I love you deeply. Of course, I'll marry you."

He took her hand and gently placed a gorgeous, $144,000 diamond engagement ring on her finger. "I love you! Thank you for agreeing to be my wife. I will do everything in my power to make you happy every minute, every hour, every day."

They embraced and kissed with great emotion. At that moment, it did not matter to them where they were or who was watching. At that moment, only Dr. Benson and Olivia exist.

4

The newly engaged couple continued to walk around the greenhouse. Dr. Benson wrote down a list of plants that he believed to have pharmaceutical potential. Time was of the essence, and he knew it was going to be another all-nighter in the laboratory. He needed some energy. He looked at his watch—it was time to go.

"Olivia, may we leave and get a cup of joe?" he asks.

"Yes, please, my handsome fiancé."

They asked the gardener to place the plants and flowers Dr. Benson had noted down in the Mercedes, then Robert spent a few more moments with Mr. Hughes.

"I received a good variety of plants for my extracting experiments," he said. "Thank you, Mr. Hughes. But I must leave now."

Mr. Hughes nodded. "I can see in your eyes a burning desire to find a cure for cancer. I won't take any more of your valuable time. Good-bye, Ms. Olivia. Dr. Benson, I know you will succeed."

They shook hands, and then Dr. Benson and Olivia moved toward the Mercedes.

"May I drive, Robert? I want to drive you up and down."

"Your pleasure is my pleasure, my beautiful angel." He handed her the keys and held the driver's door open. They gazed into each other's eyes for a moment, burning with love. Then Dr. Benson got into the passenger seat. "Let's go," he says. "I can see clearly the trees through the forest, my love."

She smiled. "And I can hear clearly the trees through the forest, which is your heart pounding with love for me."

They drove away from John Hughes's estate. Olivia put some romantic classical music on low and began to rev the engine hard, speeding but still maintaining control of the Mercedes. Dr. Benson leaned over and kissed her cheek. He felt like God himself must have sent Olivia to be his wife; they were so compatible. He looked at the sky and said, "Thank you, God!"

She pulled into a little café overlooking a lake. Many couples went here to drink coffee or hot chocolate while they had romantic conversations. Olivia and Dr. Benson held hands, kissed, and talked about their future while they drank their cups of joe and enjoyed the view of the lake. They spent a few hours there, but it seemed like only minutes to them.

One of the waitresses noticed Olivia's purse and asked where she got it. Olivia smiled. "I purchased this purse in Paris when I traveled there, thank you."

Dr. Benson stepped in. "My fiancée is a ballerina, and she travels many places."

"Wow, I knew there was something special about you," the waitress said. "I've brought you both a special dessert to go with your coffee. On the house, you two lovebirds!"

"Thank you!" they say.

After they ate the dessert and had another cup of joe each, Olivia said, "It's time we should go. I'm worried about father. Is there anything you can tell me about his health?"

Dr. Benson knows she is attempting to pick his brain for medical information about Adolfo. He says quickly, "Your father has a heart of courage and honor. Please don't worry. Trust me, I'm a doctor."

He signaled for the waitress, who has not bothered them so they could have quality romantic time. Before she can give him the bill, however, he hands her one Benjamin and says, "This is for the excellent coffee, and for your pleasant service. God bless you!"

The cute little waitress's eyes light up. "Thank you, sir, and God bless you both, too!"

Dr. Benson escorted Olivia to the car.

"I'm driving, Robert! I need to!" she says. He looked at her lovely smile and knew she was very happy.

"Test what's under the hood and enjoy!" As they get in, he turns on the stereo. He programs it to play celestial music, his favorite. When he listens to celestial, he always feels that God has truly blessed him.

Olivia was clearly having enormous fun as she flew down the road. She drove so fast, Dr. Benson checked his seat belt a couple of times just to be sure it was fastened. He knows he can't find a cure for cancer if he doesn't stay alive!

The sun was going down as they pulled up the driveway of Adolfo's house. Dr. Benson got out of the car to open her door, like a gentleman. "May I escort you to the front door, my elegant lady?"

"Yes, please!" Olivia returned his car keys, and he walked her to the door.

"May I see you in a couple of days?" he asked. "My father, the army general, is coming home to visit. It would be an honor if you would meet him."

"Yes, of course!" she said as they kissed each other good-bye.

—⁓—

As Olivia entered her father's house, she placed her hand in her pocket so her father could not see the diamond ring on her finger.

"Please sit down, Father," she says. "Would you tell me how you met Mother?"

"We met while on a ballet tour," Adolfo responded. "She was dancing in her native England, and I was on tour there. I remember she danced with such grace, though she was not as athletic as you, my precious Olivia."

Then she showed Adolfo her hand. He jumped from his chair and they hugged, her tears of joy falling all over him.

"Congratulations, my darling!" he says. "Wait here. I have something for you from your beautiful mother, God rest her soul." He went up into the attic and returned with a dress box.

Olivia opened it and found an exquisite white wedding dress. She wept as she said, "Mother, thank you. It's the most beautiful dress I have ever seen." She hugged Adolfo again and they cried together; both wished her mother was still with them, and had not died of cancer.

5

At an afternoon ballet performance several days later, Dr. Benson and his father, General Arnold Benson, are seated in the front row. A large group of dancers, both men and women, came onto the stage leaping and spinning, followed by the star ballerina—Olivia.

"Look, Father! That's my fiancée, Olivia."

The general watched in amazement as the elegant young lady began with an arabesque, her body supported on one leg, the other extended straight behind her. Then she performed several grand pas de chats, large steps that showcased why she was the lead dancer. Suddenly she trots briskly, then leaps extremely high over the other dancers, performing a grand jeté with extraordinary showmanship. She blended her moves with the sounds of the beautiful music. She leapt, spun in a pirouette, and smiled at the audience without even gasping for air.

As the general watched he said, "Wow! Amazing! Erstaunlich! I don't follow ballet, but is she famous, son?"

"Yes, she is the best in the world! Father, you still throw in some German words when you're in conversation? I miss mother, too!" The general remembers his deceased beloved German wife, and periodically speaks German to remember her.

"There's nothing wrong in remembering the past, son, but she could be a super soldier if she wanted to be. She is so athletic and graceful, for what the United States military could do with her skills?" The general looks at the ballerina in pleased astonishment.

And Dr. Benson says, "Father, her talent was meant to bring goodness and beauty to the world, not destruction."

Suddenly Olivia glided and spun toward Dr. Benson. She stopped right in front of him and made a courtesy bow to the audience, but while looking into his eyes. The harmonious classical music continued to play in the background. Dr. Benson ached to hold her. Even the audience seemed to feel their chemistry.

He handed her a single large rose and smiled. "I love you, Olivia!" he said.

A tear trickled down her face, and she wiped it away gently with the rose. Then she smiled at the audience and performed several slow final pirouettes to display her athleticism. She slowly came to a stop and opened her arms.

The other dancers glided toward Olivia on their knees and stopped to form a circle around her, the prima ballerina, to honor her. She made her final bow, signaling that the show was over. The audience gave a loud standing ovation in joyous appreciation, clapping until their hands were sore.

6

A few months pass. Dr. Benson discovers that one of the plants from John Hughes's greenhouse reacted strangely when he accidentally spilled hot coffee on it. He wondered if he could extract the plant's enzymes to add to his cancer medication. It was the plant Mr. Hughes said came possibly from the time of Noah.

Dr. Benson and Olivia Newton are scheduled to be married the following Saturday at a Catholic church in Beverly Hills. The wedding invitations were sent out months ago. They have invited famous actors and actresses from the United States, Mexico, England, France, Italy, Canada, Germany, China, and Japan. There will also be famous athletes from the United States, France, Spain, the Philippines, Mexico, Canada, and several European countries. Royal guests from all over the world, including the Middle East, England, France, Spain, Greece, and Italy, will also attend. To Dr.

Benson, however, the most important guests will be his adored father and his colleagues of fellow physicians, biochemists, and biologists. The guests Olivia most wants to see are her father and their ballet and opera family. A famous female opera singer friend of Olivia's will perform as a wedding gift to her. The number of attendees was large, because people wanted to honor the Nobel Prize–winning Dr. Benson for his herbal medicines, which had helped so many of them achieve better health. He is somewhat on the young side, yet he has accomplished unbelievable success.

On the day of the wedding, Dr. Benson had entered the church alone, wearing an exquisitely tailored tuxedo. He wished to God his mother could be there. Standing alone at the altar before the ceremony was to begin, he had looked straight up through the open ceiling window. He viewed the sky filled with white doves above and said, "God, please let my Olivia be my savior now that my mother is gone!" He couldn't help but tear up. He felt so nervous standing there as he waited for his bride to enter the church. Dr. Benson thought about their upcoming plans. He and Olivia had agreed that, immediately after the ceremony, they would fly to Hawaii for their honeymoon. They decided not to have a reception right away, but to hold a grand ball to celebrate sometime after they returned instead. These plans would allow him to focus on finding a cure for cancer for a while longer, fulfilling the promise he made to his mother. Dr. Benson felt enormously grateful that his father would be there, though, serving as best man and overseeing security. General Benson was a proper man who spread good values. Dr. Benson hoped his father would stay and retire from the military.

General Benson entered the church wearing his formal military uniform. The marriage was to be performed by the Pope himself, another patient of Dr. Benson's. It was a well-known fact that Dr. Benson had cured the pope's arthritis, Parkinson's, and Alzheimer's. The pope had been in the area to see the doctor, and when he learned of his upcoming marriage, he offered to preside over the wedding. The pope believed that Dr. Benson was sent by God to help cure people, so he wanted to bless the couple personally. The pope proclaims that Dr. Benson's actions speak for itself, as he says, "Res ispa locuitur!"

—⁂—

At last, the ceremony began. Dr. Benson was filled with awe and happiness as the famous opera singer performed "Ave Maria." The bride looked beautiful as she strode up the aisle, escorted by her father. When they reached the altar, Adolfo said to Dr. Benson, "Please take care of my daughter!"

"With all my heart! All my life!" Dr. Benson promised. He smiled to reassure them of his honesty, and to show them the esteem he had for both of them.

The pope lit incense in a small gold box and said a blessing over it. He held the box by a thin gold chain and swung it gently in all directions, then gave it to one of the altar boys. The pungent aroma of burning incense filled the church as the altar boys carried the box up and down the aisles.

When the music ended, the pope began to speak about how man and woman, beginning with Adam and Eve and then Robert and Olivia, were God's natural creations. Only when they were joined together could man and woman create life. Suddenly, two peaceful white doves landed on a ledge near one of the church's front windows. The pope saw the two doves and smiled as if he knew the meaning of their arrival. His face gleamed with peace eternal as he continued the ceremony.

Angelo, a Beverly Hills world traveler news photographer and friend of Olivia's, is there for her, and to film the pope. Suddenly, Angelo sees General Benson—someone he remembers from the war—and high fives him.

"It's a small world, huh, General?" Angelo says.

"Yes it is, Angelo. I'm surprised to see you here? I thought they killed you in the war you crazy SOB with all that gun-fire all around."

Angelo is the professional photographer that has been granted exclusive coverage of the ceremony. He is also taping and photographing the wedding for Dr. Benson and Olivia. When Dr. Benson tried to insist on paying Angelo for his services, Angelo just laughed.

"Indeed, you will-with front-row seats to the next ballet performance! I promised three persons. Me! Myself! And I!" Angelo, who is also gay, laughed. Angelo has overcome many adversities and toured several wars as a freelance photographer, which won him the Pulitzer Prize. But Angelo is more grateful that he was able to save some children from heavy gunfire, which came from both sides. A bullet has no friends, Angelo would say to himself as he put his life on the line to rescue many children.

Unfortunately, Angelo's life does have a saddened past that he has never gotten over. Angelo suffered a trauma when he was only eight years old. He witnessed his older brother, David, who was thirteen years old then, drown in the Rio Grande River, on a dare from other children to cross it, which some of them were first cousins. He remembers shouting, "Stop! Help my brother!" Angelo cried with fear as he attempted in vain—to get into the water himself—to somehow grab his big brother. Unfortunately, Angelo could not swim. Fear stopped him too as he swallowed some river water while he heard the children laughing. His loving sole brother splashed helplessly, while the river's powerful underneath currents took him under to his death. Angelo never really got over this. He still, even as an adult, has not learned to swim. And he stays away from rivers, beaches, and pools. Angelo blamed his parents for leaving him and his big brother for the weekend in the care of an irresponsible aunt and uncle, who lived by the Rio Grande River, and drank from their homemade moonshine, white lightning, mountain dew hooch liquor all day long. Angelo grew up with parents who just liked to party and never went to church. The only person that took care of Angelo was his big brother, David, who no longer exists. Angelo's parents never kept watchful eyes on their children. Thus, they lost their first-born son, David, who was liked by all and was a heterosexual with a nice loving girlfriend.

Angelo emotionally wipes a few tears off his eyes then takes a photograph as Dr. Benson held Olivia's hand. When the pope asked if he wished to marry her, for better or for worse, till death, he said, "I do!"

The pope asked Olivia the same. "Yes, I do, with all my heart," she answered.

The pope asked the general for the rings. When he opened the box, Dr. Benson saw his mother's wedding ring in it. It's an Egyptian artifact of pure gold with engravings of flowers and the Nile River circling a big blue diamond. General Benson had obtained the ring when he served in the Middle East. Dr. Benson looked at him in disbelief.

"It's all right, son," his father assured him. "This way, your mother is here too!"

As Dr. Benson took the ring, the pope said, "If anyone objects to this holy marriage—between man and woman—Robert Benson and Olivia Newton, speak now or forever hold your peace." The attendees were silent. The pope made a Christian blessing in the name of Jesus then instructed Dr. Benson to place the ring on Olivia's finger. "I now pronounce you husband and wife. With God's blessing, may your matrimony be long and forever joyful. You may now kiss the bride."

Dr. Benson gently lifted the delicate veil from over Olivia's face and looked deep into her eyes. He took her in his arms and kissed her deeply as the church bells rang and people cheered. Angelo, flashing photographs of the newlyweds, suddenly embraces his friend Olivia and says with tears, "Please take care of your children! Keep a watchful eye on them and don't leave them with just anybody. No matter if they are family. Children should only be left with proven responsible people." Olivia knows that Dr. Benson and Angelo invite comparison by having a traumatic childhood tragedy. Someone—perhaps their loved one—died in front of their eyes, which changed the outcome of their life. Dr. Benson, however, feels he was benefited by at least having his father to guide and take care of him. Unfortunately, Angelo did not, his parents were never around. And when they were, they ridiculed Angelo by saying to him he should have been the one who drowned. Olivia, with tears streaming down her face, and Dr. Benson smiling jubilantly, reach out and embrace Angelo. They both say simultaneously to their friend, "Thank you, Angelo. May the Lord watch over you now, Angelo, our good friend!"

As they exited the church, the guests tossed rice at them. Dr. Benson saw John Hughes in the crowd.

"Have fun in Hawaii, Dr. Benson!" he called. "Everything has been arranged!" John Hughes shouts. And Angelo, with tears in both eyes, takes a memorable photo of the newlyweds, and waves goodbye! Then Dr. Benson, seeing his father standing at attention looking at him and holding a military salute, returns a salute back to the general. Olivia, however, has only eyes for her husband, Dr. Robert Benson. They continue shuffling down the beautiful Roman marble steps.

The limousine was waiting. The chauffeur opened the door, saying, "Congratulations, Dr. and Mrs. Benson!" They smiled at him, at a loss for words, and climbed in. The limousine was filled with flower petals, and its exterior was decorated with bells and flowers. Dr. Benson took Olivia's hand and kissed her strikingly beautiful wedding ring, thinking of his late mother.

They noticed a bottle wrapped up with a bow. A note said it was from General Benson. Dr. Benson read it aloud. "Robert, please enjoy this red wine from Domaine de la Romanée-Conti. I picked it up for you in Vosne-Romanée, France. Genießen! Enjoy every moment with your wife. She is an angel. Remember, son, all you will have at the end of your life will be memories, so fill your days with memories of your family. I have lived every day like it could be my last, and now your mother still lives inside me because of those memories. Even though you are a busy doctor and scientist, always put your family first. Your father, General Arnold Benson. PS I want grandchildren!"

Dr. Benson thought to himself about starting to amass memories right then. He poured them both a glass of wine and made a toast. "You know, red wine has resveratrol, which is good for long life. I want to live a long time to be with you, Olivia. Drink up!" They kissed and enjoyed their ride to the airport.

—◊—

The plane ride seemed to take no time at all. As the commercial jet suddenly descended from the clouds like a huge bird, Dr. Benson and Olivia looked out the window. They could see palm trees, flowers, sandy beaches, and ocean vistas.

"This must be Hawaii," she said. "It looks like the garden of Eden!"

It was late afternoon when they checked into their villa on a beach, a honeymoon gift from John Hughes. They were hungry, so they dined outside, just in time to participate in a Hawaiian luau. Dr. Benson quickly rubbed on some sunblock over his face, arms, and legs to prevent skin cancer.

Olivia said, "Let's go, Robert!" They arrived to a beautiful island setting were muscular Hawaiian men danced with torches and beautiful Hawaiian women shook their curvy bodies to the beat of drums. A huge pig wrapped in leaves was being roasted over a pit of red-hot coals. It smelled delicious.

Dr. Benson gazed at his wife. She looked splendid in a white beach dress she had purchased in Madrid. It showed off her athletic figure and beautiful profile.

The hostess—a gorgeous, full-figured Hawaiian girl in her midtwenties—came over to them and said, "Welcome to Hawaii! My name is Hu'elani." She placed leis around their necks and then hugged and kissed them. Dr. Benson noticed that when Hu'elani kissed him on the cheek, she seemed to smell his neck. Then she looked right into his eyes; he thought he could see desire in them.

Olivia and Dr. Benson sat down on bamboo mats, as instructed by the waitress. They feasted their eyes on the Hawaiian food laid out in front of them like a buffet—kalua pig, moa chicken, whitefish filets, lomi-lomi salmon, barbecue shrimp, and crab legs. Dr. Benson personally preferred sushi and mariscos; but since they were not available, he started with poke, raw fish marinated in lemon juice and coconut cream and served with seaweed and onions. He thought it was delicious.

Olivia began with lomi-lomi salmon and poi. "Have some," she said. "It's made from taro root and is good for your health. It's delicious."

"If you love it, then I've got to try a big portion!"

"You asked for it!" She put a big bite in his mouth and prevented him from spitting it out by kissing him.

There were plenty more fruits and green vegetable salads to try. Dr. Benson perused the selection of mangoes, bananas, pineapples, and coconuts. All were sweet, he thought, but not as sweet as his wife's kisses.

Night fell, and the luau came to an end. Dr. Benson and Olivia walked hand in hand on the beach, admiring the reflection of the full moon on the lovely blue ocean water.

"I love you," he said. "I wish we could live forever."

"Our love will live forever, Robert, through our children," Olivia said.

They kissed to the sound of the waves caressing the sand. Then they returned to their villa.

"No alcohol on our honeymoon night, please!" she says.

Dr. Benson liked the sound of that. He didn't enjoy drinking too much alcohol anyway. "No, of course! Your restraint is one of the many reasons why I love you."

"Our love is true. I want to feel your heart, pure and clear, all night long!" Outside a huge window that overlooked the beach, they could see the moonlight reflected on the ocean and hear the water pounding the shore, which stirred their passion. They begin to hug and kiss while taking their clothes off. They soon found themselves on a huge, king-sized bed. An island idol stood next to it, apparently blessing them with Hawaii's power and beauty. A bamboo table next to it held a huge bowl full of assorted fresh fruit, several pitchers of water and drinking glasses. They made passionate love all night, stopping only to eat some fruit and drink some water for energy.

—⚬—

It was afternoon when they awoke in each other's arms. The plentiful fruit was gone, and only one pitcher of water remained to drink. Dr. Benson poured some for each of them and said, "Salute to our marriage, my beautiful Olivia! May we live forever and ever!"

"And may we be blessed with loving, healthy children!"

Her English accent fired him up. They toasted and made passionate love again and again. Afterward, they lay in bed talking, feeling open to one another. Dr. Benson wanted to shake off his drowsiness, though, so they could make more memories together that day. They went for a breath of fresh air as they got a ride on a rickshaw. The muscular native Hawaiian tour guide pulled them around the Island on a two-wheeled rickshaw. The wild boar, sheep, and deer ran by as they heard birds singing in the near distance. As the sun shone, a few drops of rain came down on them. As the tour guide slowed to a trot, pulling the rickshaw, they saw beautiful tropical flowers with water falling into a pond as colorful fish splashed. Olivia and Dr. Benson felt as if they were in the Garden of Eden. As they moved on from the tropical paradise, they viewed the powerful volcano rumbling as they held each other. After a peaceful moment, the powerful Hawaiian tour guide pulled the rickshaw back to the villa. Dr. Benson assisted his beautiful wife, Olivia, off the rickshaw.

"Do you want to go out for some tea or a cup of joe?" he asked.

"A cup of joe, of course."

At the villa restaurant, Olivia simply glowed. The waitresses and waiters were clearly in awe of her beauty. They couple sat down and ordered Hawaiian coffee.

"Good cup of joe!" she declared.

Then a small voice from a nearby tree branch repeated, "Good cup of joe!"

They looked to see a parrot moving up and down the branch. Olivia said, "What a clever bird! I sure would love to have a bird like that."

A waiter overheard them. "Mr. Hughes, the owner of this villa, brought the parrot here with his wife a few years ago when it was just a baby," he explained. "But when Mrs. Hughes died of cancer, he left the parrot here at the villa."

"Mr. Hughes is my friend and patient! I'm Dr. Benson. Are you sure no one here owns the bird?"

"No, Mr. Hughes just abandoned Herbie there. That bird has no more owner than you do, Dr. Benson, sir."

"He does now!" Dr. Benson says. He took out his cell phone and dialed. "Mr. Hughes, this is Dr. Benson. I have a question, sir."

"Okay, Dr. Benson," Dr. Hughes responded on the other end of the line. "Who told you I haven't exercised all week? And that I went on a chocolate-eating craze?"

He laughed. "No, Mr. Hughes, that is not why I am calling. But we will have to address what you just said when I get back from my honeymoon!"

"I was just kidding, Dr. Benson. I just wanted to throw a little humor at you. Now, what is your question?"

"There is a parrot named Herbie living here at your villa. I was wondering if I could buy him from you."

"Dr. Benson, the bird is yours for free. I will tell the villa manager to hand Herbie's ownership papers and records over to you. And by the way, I have complete confidence that when you come home, you'll find a cure for cancer in no time."

"I appreciate your confidence, Mr. Hughes. There is nothing I want more in this life than to find that cure. And you will certainly be one of the first people to receive my treatment."

"Thank you, Doctor. Enjoy the rest of your honeymoon, and I'll see you soon. Good-bye now."

"Good-bye, Mr. Hughes, and thank you for Herbie!"

Olivia and Dr. Benson were still finishing their savory Hawaiian coffee when the manager came over. "Dr. Benson, I was just ordered by Mr. Hughes to give you all of Herbie's paperwork. Rest assured, the bird will be brought to you for safe travel."

"Thank you, sir!" Dr. Benson said.

They finished their coffee and got up from the table. As they were passing the pool, the hostess from the previous evening, Hu'elani, walked up to them, carrying Herbie in a travel cage.

"I understand you will be leaving Hawaii in a few hours," she said. "Here is your new pet. Now, before you go, can I give you a big, friendly, Hawaiian kiss good-bye?"

"You will not kiss my Robert, so back off, Hoe'elani!" Olivia suddenly exclaimed in a fit of jealousy.

"My name is Hu'elani! Please say it correctly! Don't worry. This is just the traditional Hawaiian way of saying good-bye so you will return. Now pucker up, good-looking doctor! I have desired to give you a huge delicious kiss since the luau. It's Hawaii's tradition and my pleasure!"

As she moved to kiss him on the lips, Olivia grabbed her. Though Hu'elani was in physically good condition and could put up a minor struggle, she was no match for Olivia's athletic muscles. Using the same concentration of mind, muscle, and balance she drew upon on stage, Olivia tossed Hu'elani in the pool.

"Wow," Dr. Benson said, holding Herbie's cage.

"Wow!" Herbie squawked, and then whistled appreciatively at the cat fight between the two beautiful athletic women.

"Oh, Robert, what have I done?" Olivia fretted.

Dr. Benson laughed. "It's only human nature, my love, human nature."

Soon after, they departed Hawaii on a first-class flight back to Los Angeles.

7

Several months later, Dr. Benson and Olivia held the wedding ball they had planned. There were only a few guests at their mansion. No liquor was served, only freshly squeezed fruit juice. Famous actors and actresses, physicians, and ballet friends attended the reception held in the house's main ballroom.

"Where is the liquor?" asked one of the actors.

"I'm an herbalist, remember?" Dr. Benson said. "I believe in good health."

Another actor and actress came to his defense. "We are herbalists too, and we believe in health, music, and a lot of dancing!"

Everybody enjoyed the delicious catered food.

A famous singer opened up the celebration with a song. It was one of Dr. Benson's favorites. "May we dance?" he asked his wife.

"Anything for you, my love!"

He sang softly in her ear as they danced. She kissed him and then placed her nose on his neck. She could smell his cologne.

The next number was sung by a famous country singer, and everyone danced along with a two-step. It was followed by a rapper. Finally, the ballet dancers performed. Olivia joined them, spinning and jumping high in the air as only a ballerina can. There was huge applause. At the end of the evening, Olivia and Dr. Benson thanked everyone for coming and said good-bye.

A few days later, Olivia discovered she was pregnant. She hurried through the house, looking for her husband. She found him making notes and drinking a cup of joe in the study.

"Robert, will you walk with me? I have some news that affects us both," she asked.

He put his important research notes in a waterproof carrying case and locked it to secure his documents. He left it on his desk and stood up. "This sounds important."

They walked out into the garden, holding hands. Dr. Benson knew that Olivia had been feeling nauseous lately, and he had been worried about her. He admired how her discomfort had not kept her from constructing a beautiful garden in their spacious backyard, though.

Dr. Benson plucked an apple off a tree, rubbed it on his shirt, and took a bite. Olivia smelled the apple.

"Mmm, Robert!" she says.

Dr. Benson raised the apple to Olivia's lips. She bit off a small portion then squeezed his hand.

"I'm pregnant, Robert. It's a boy."

He softly dropped the apple. It hit the ground and rolled into a nearby fish pound with a splash.

"Olivia!" he cried as they hugged and kissed. "How far along are you?"

"I have been pregnant for months, but I did not know. My gynecologist says many women are different, and she believes it was due to my very good athletic condition that I was not aware I was pregnant. I believe we are having a little angel sent to us from God."

"You are an angel, too, my darling, and now God has sent us a little boy angel. Trust me, I'm a doctor."

—ɷ—

Olivia was under instruction from her doctor not to exert herself by performing ballet, but was also told that walking or using a stationary bike would be good preparation for her upcoming labor.

When her due date approached, Dr. Benson gave her a pager to carry at all times.

"Thank you for caring," she told him. "I will just stay around the house, working on my garden. It smells so wonderful!"

"It sure does. I can smell it from our bedroom balcony." He looked at his watch. "Honey, I have an appointment. Will you come back inside with me?"

"Let me see something in my garden first. I will be in shortly!"

Dr. Benson knew how much his wife loved her garden. She had filled it with flowers, rare plants, fruit trees, and various vegetables. Olivia used no pesticides, only organic gardening techniques. It had been a lot of work to create, but Adolfo helped her. The only thing Dr. Benson contributed to the garden was a well to provide them with fresh drinking water. A friend had surveyed the land and discovered a deep natural water source on the grounds. Dr. Benson had also had a deck built and covered it with solar panels to draw energy from the sun, but he didn't stop there. He had a tower built with a windmill to draw energy from air. He was very pleased that came with knowing a self-sufficient natural energy source would power his experiments. He later had a powerful generator installed in his garage and connected it to the entire estate just to ensure that the house and laboratory would always have energy in case the solar panels or windmill failed in some way.

He gazed around at the backyard. He felt blessed. Then he went back inside, to the bedroom. Herbie the parrot flew out onto the balcony, all around the grounds, and then back inside. He sometimes liked to hide and listen to conversations. He always surprised Dr. Benson with his stealth and amused him by repeating words he'd overheard.

Dr. Benson stepped inside his walk-in closet. He was about to get dressed to give a lecture on cancer treatments and possible cures at a seminar in Beverly Hills. Scientists, physicians, biologists, and politicians from all over the world would be there.

"Can I help you, my dear?" Olivia had snuck up on him with her soft footsteps.

"Of course!" he says. They browsed through his thirty suits, sports coats, dinner jackets, and golf suits. She chose a blue English suit, a blue shirt, and a blue tie.

"Now go to your seminar, my love. You look brilliantly distinguished!"

They kissed passionately. "I shall return soon!" Dr. Benson promised. They kissed some more, and then he left for the seminar.

He arrived early at the auditorium. He saw many familiar, and some unfamiliar, faces passing through metal detectors by the entrance. All attendees and their personal bags were thoroughly inspected for any weapons. He noticed that people seemed to be talking about him and pointing toward him. It did not bother him.

It was soon time to begin. Everyone who was somebody was there. The British prime minister, the president of the United States, and leaders from Japan, China, Russia, the Middle East, Germany, France, Italy, Israel, Mexico, Spain, Canada, and South Africa. To Dr. Benson, however, the most important people in the audience were his cancer patients and colleagues—physicians, scientists, and biochemists.

"Ladies, gentlemen, countrymen, and colleagues, thank you for coming," he began. "My name is Dr. Robert Benson. I am a physician and biologist conducting scientific research in a quest to cure cancer. Everyone here will feel my enthusiasm and burning desire to find this cure. I want each of you to know how honored I feel to be standing before you so many fine people. I also want you to know that the time is near when no one will need to fear ill health or the loss of a loved one to cancer any longer. I am close to finding a cure. I will demonstrate to all of you some of my medical discoveries!"

Dr. Benson picked several volunteers at random to come up on stage. They suffered from different ailments, none of which had been disclosed to him. He began to examine them in front of everyone, using his thumb to open their eyes. Just by looking at the coloring and spots on the whites of their eyes or their pupils' size and coloring, he is able to develop an initial prognosis. He announced each individual's disease.

"Gastritis."

"Asthma."

"Liver weakness, possibly cancer."

"Heart weakness, with the possible risk of a stroke in the future."

"Immune system failure, possible HIV."

Suddenly a man jumped up from the audience and cried out, "This is the devil's work! You need to stop what you're doing or you'll be stopped by someone permanently! You do not belong in this world! You must die!"

The Beverly Hills police and federal agents quickly grabbed the man and escorted him out of the auditorium in handcuffs. Later, Dr. Benson heard that the officers discovered an unlawful concealed fiberglass handgun loaded with fiberglass bullets on the man. Somehow he had evaded the metal detectors. The firearm was confiscated by authorities, and the man was charged with violating the following three California Penal Codes: Section 12025 carrying a concealed firearm, Section 12031 carrying a loaded firearm, and Section 422 criminal threats orally specific and unequivocal to Dr. Benson in front of many witnesses.

In the meantime, however, Dr. Benson shouted for order and continued with his lecture. "Concentration and creative vision keep me focused on my quest to cure all cancers. I believe we can all see the trees for the forest. I want to increase longevity. I want us all to live two hundred years and enjoy our parents, children, and children's children. I believe an average person shouldn't die an early death. I believe a person should have time to himself after working all his life, that he should have time to enjoy family more, travel more, and be at peace. If individuals throughout the world are at harmony and peace, there will be less mistrust among us. We could see an end to war, nor would any wars be necessary.

"First of all, cancer known medically as a malignant neoplasm, is a broad group of diseases involving unregulated cell growth. Cancer cells which are abnormal cells that divide and grow uncontrollably, forming malignant tumors that are full of circulating tumor cells. If a person disrupts their healthy normal cell balance, consequently they are at risk of acquiring cancer. All humans should live a healthy lifestyle to impede of ever acquiring cancer. This means eating plenty of fresh raw fruits, fresh raw vegetables, less, or no meats, and drink plenty of water to keep their digestive system clean. Exercise is important, and it does not matter if you have a disability. Creatively, there exist some form of exercise you can do, with effort. Of course, a person must not partake in any vices such as non-prescription drugs, consuming alcohol, or inhaling smoke products of any kind. These unnatural, unregulated vices will disrupt the normal cells' healthy balance. Furthermore, stress and unhappiness can also disrupt the normal cells' healthy balance." Dr. Benson pauses to drink some water.

"Dear kind ladies and honorable brave gentleman. Please listen carefully. I must inform you that cancer can be caused by a germ or a virus. This means something subcellular in the human body can remain dormant, but can unfortunately be suddenly triggered in a number of ways to become cancerous. Now I want to discuss my ideas about a cure for cancer. Circulating tumor cells often break away from a primary tumor site where a person has cancer. In other words, if we can contain the initial site of cancer in your breast, liver, lungs, brain, pancreas, colon, prostate, skin, bone, or blood, the abnormal cancerous cells will not spread throughout your body like seeds to metastasize and kill you. Imiquimod, a drug already on the market, in combination with Metformin, a diabetes medication derived from a natural source and consumed daily along with my new sleep medication, will slow down your cancer.

"I am now working on a cancer-destroying medication that I believe can completely cure cancer, in all its forms. It's based on supercharged granulocyte immune cells. These immune cells are specifically designed to kill cancer cells without killing normal cells. So far, however, I have only cured rodents and other animals. There still is a missing link with humans. I can only get human cancer cells to go into remission so far. The cancer always comes back eventually."

Suddenly an arrogant, unhappy woman physician who was crying stood up and shouted, "I lost my mom to cancer!" Immediately a group of fellow physicians and scientists embraced her with compassion. Dr. Benson's own eyes watered up as he remembered his own mother, Mary. He paused for a drink of water as people began to raise their hands and shout out questions.

"There are two hundred plus types of cancer, and different forms of cancers are on the rise in the human population. Many cancers are based on a virus, like the human immunodeficiency virus or the acquired immunodeficiency syndrome, which spreads in the human body almost without control. They use people as hosts and can hide in reservoirs of the body. I have studied monkeys and cats that live with the HIV to find out how to possibly cure cancer." Suddenly a saddened look comes across Dr. Bensons face. "In the past, I made a promise to my beloved mother that I will eradicate cancer!"

The president of the United States raised his hand high to ask a question. "I believe in change, and curing and preventing cancer will surely change the world. But how do we communicate this news to the masses?"

"Brilliant question, Mr. President," Dr. Benson responded. "Yes, we humans should change our lifestyle to vastly reduce the risk of ever acquiring cancer. Finally and to conclude my presentation. In the near future, the human race should have one universal language, which should be taught at all schools throughout the world. Remember the story of the Tower of Babel? All people spoke one language before that. Their communication was so good, they were almost able to work together to reach the heavens. I believe that by using the mind, everything is possible. With good communication and imagination, we could again reach the heavens."

Dr. Benson received a loud standing ovation.

8

In the next morning's newspaper, Dr. Benson saw an article about his speech.

"The lecture on cancer, given by local physician and biologist Dr. Robert Benson, was amazingly informative. Benson is highly regarded for his research on curing diseases, and he won the Nobel Prize for curing arthritis, Parkinson's, and Alzheimer's. His current research focuses on all forms of cancers as well as the AIDS virus. Benson's wife, Olivia, is a world-class ballerina from England."

After Dr. Benson finished reading the paper—while drinking a cup of joe—he said to himself with a smile, "Wow! My wife wasn't even at the seminar, and she got her name in print? Human beings are incredible! I think I'll switch to my computer to help my research."

Olivia had not come downstairs yet. She had been sleeping more due to her pregnancy, and Dr. Benson didn't wish to wake her. She could go into labor any day. He had been staying home more often to be near her, but he continued his research. He had been reading all the medical journals on the latest developments in cancer research.

He went to his study to do some reading. He knew that when Olivia woke up, she would probably visit her garden before eating breakfast. She loved to observe its running brook, its fish, its flowers, and its various fruit trees. If she was hungry, she could simply pick a fruit of her choice right off the branch. The smell of the garden had a calming effect on her, she told him.

Dr. Benson was jotting down notes in his study when suddenly his pager went off. He raced to the bedroom, but Olivia was not there. He ran to the garden, where he found her lying in yerba buena next to a fragrant honeysuckle. She was moaning. He took his cell phone from his pocket and called 911. The paramedics arrived almost immediately, evaluated his wife's situation, and said, "We have to take her to the hospital right away!"

Dr. Benson climbed into the ambulance with Olivia. On their way to the hospital, one of the paramedics in the back asked, "Would you like a cup of joe, Dr. Benson?"

"Yes, please," he said and then took a sip. "Wow, this is a great cup of joe!"

"I like the smell of your cup of joe, honey. It makes me feel comfortable," Olivia murmured. "May I drink some?"

"I don't know…what do you think, Dr. Benson?" a paramedic asked.

"Sure, darling, but only a little sip," he said. "And don't worry, gentlemen, coffee is alkaline, which is good for the blood."

The paramedic nodded. "Yes, that's right, coffee comes from the coffee bean. We know that you know a lot about medicinal plants, Doctor."

The paramedic who was driving turned on a classical radio station for a little music. A song about an angel happened to be on.

As Olivia breathed through her contractions, Dr. Benson suddenly had a strong feeling that angels from heaven were inside the ambulance with them.

Then Olivia cried out, "The baby's coming now!"

Moments later, she pushed, and a baby boy came into the world smoothly, thanks to her athletic physique.

The paramedic cleaned up the baby while Olivia smiled and said, "Cup of joe, please, Robert?"

He gave her more coffee. Then the paramedic placed the baby in her arms, and she put the infant to her breast.

"Congratulations," the paramedic said. Then he took a sip of his own cup of joe. "What are you nice folks going to name him?"

Olivia looked jubilantly at her husband. "Look at him, honey. He's a little angel. How does Joe sound?"

Dr. Benson laughed as he too drank from his cup of joe. "Joe is perfect!"

They soon arrived at the hospital. The baby hadn't cried much—he rather seemed to enjoy the ride. It almost looked like he was cracking a smile, and his eyes shone with happiness. It was such a proud moment. At the hospital, a pediatrician who happened to be a friend of Dr. Benson's evaluated little Joe while Olivia's obstetrician evaluated her. Mother and child both received a good health report.

"Robert, where is my cigar? You have a nice healthy boy!" the pediatrician asked.

"I do owe you a good cigar," Dr. Benson agreed. "I've got a good connection to get some, my father!"

They spent one day and night in the hospital for observation. Dr. Benson pulled up a chair next to Olivia's bed in their private room. The chair could recline to lie flat, but he knew he wouldn't sleep a wink. He thought he would most likely drink cup after cup of joe all night. He was so happy for Olivia, himself, and their new son, Joe!

9

Several years passed, Dr. Benson continued his research. He routinely tested his cancer patients to see how many tumor cells were circulating in their blood. He had still only been able to cure rodents and other animals of cancer—no humans yet.

Adolfo looked worse now. He felt ill every day. Olivia still did not know about his cancer, because he continued to hide it from her with medication that made him able to function. Dr. Benson wanted to tell her the truth, but Adolfo had made him promise not to. He grieved to know that Adolfo's death was near, especially when it seemed that his cure was imminent.

Dr. Benson had discovered that certain deep-ocean plants, which had been hidden under coral reefs for thousands of years, contained a special, energetic enzyme. When given to rodents and animals in combination with supercharged granulocytes, the enzyme destroyed cancer quickly. He thought that if he could get the combination of enzymes and granulocytes right, it would be the secret to curing cancer. He thought it made sense that a plant from the ocean could be the key, since the human body was roughly as salty as ocean water.

Dr. Benson was desperate to cure his father-in-law, and so he decided it was time to try some of his experimental new medication on him. He put a vial of it in his carrying case. Before he left the house, though, he spent some quality time with Olivia and Joe. As his father, the general, always said, "At the end of the day, all you have are memories, so get as many quality ones as you can, especially with your family."

The parrot, Herbie, was playing hide-and-seek with little Joe. Olivia was reading a book, but put it down when Dr. Benson approached.

She gave him some good news: she was pregnant with a baby girl! He kissed her then said he was sorry, but duty called. He had to go. His family understood.

Life as a doctor and biologist was time-consuming. Dr. Benson slept very little or not at all. His burning desire to cure cancer occupied him all the time. He was as determined as Thomas Edison, Albert Einstein, Isaac Newton, or Jonas Salk. He was sure he was on the cusp of finding the answers he was looking for.

He drove off in his Mercedes. His mission that morning was to search for people who lived in the slums, barrios, and ghettos that were suffering from cancer. He looked for people sleeping on the streets who were desperate and had no place to go for treatment. Usually, Dr. Benson made these trips at night so he would be less likely to be recognized. He needed human medical research volunteers.

He parked in a secure area near a bad part of town and started walking into the terrible neighborhood. He felt out of place. He thought ironically to himself that he was a bit like Jack the Ripper, also a doctor who went to bad neighborhoods. Dr. Benson's purpose, however, was of course to cure people, not kill them.

He heard someone coughing behind some trash cans. He looked over them and saw a man huddled there, eating dog food out of a can with a spoon. Suddenly, another man appeared from the shadows. He was wearing a green army jacket and holding a big, sharp military knife.

"Please put that Ka-Bar away, sir," Dr. Benson said hastily. "I mean you two no harm!"

"You know this knife…are you in the military?"

He smiled to put them at ease. "No, but my father is."

The man put his knife away. "What do you want around here, fancy-pants?"

"I need a medical research volunteer. I have food, hot coffee, and pastries. And medicine for coughs."

"You can't help us!" said the man in the green jacket. "My friend Pete here has liver cancer, and I got toxic blood cancer from the war in Iraq!"

"Roger," said the man with the cough, "let the man talk."

"I have medicine that may cure cancer," Dr. Benson said. "How about if we get some coffee and food and have a talk?"

They went to a grimy little restaurant nearby. Roger told Dr. Benson that, after he had been denied compensation by the military for his illness, his family no longer wanted to support him, and that the people at the veterans hospital told him to take a shower before he ever came back because he stunk. He said that even if he knew of a place where he could shower, his pride would never let him go back to that hospital.

Dr. Benson made a deal with the two men. He said that if they would agree to test this new medication as medical research volunteers, he would compensate them and pay for a motel room. This way they would have a safe place to sleep, and he could visit them and observe how the medication was working.

They agreed to the terms. They signed his medical research volunteer release and listed their next of kin and their addresses on it. As a bonus, Dr. Benson told Roger that he would ask his father to assist with a disability compensation appeal. Roger was grateful as his eyes overflowed with tears.

10

S everal months passed as Dr. Benson continued his experiments. One day, he came home from working at the hospital to find Olivia in the garden. Joe was playing with Herbie nearby.

Joe stopped at a flowering bush and inhaled deeply. "Wow, Mommy, this flower smells good!" he exclaimed.

"It smells beautiful and looks beautiful," she agreed. "It's called a rose."

"Rose!" Joe said.

"Rose! Rose! Rose!" Herbie repeated.

It was truly a beautiful family moment. Dr. Benson picked Joe up in his arms. Then he kissed Olivia and walked around the garden with her. They passed a pond filled with colorful fish and a bench by the well. A small Japanese bridge served as a walkway.

"This is a good learning moment, Joe," Dr. Benson said. He wanted to explain to Joe about searching for peace eternal within yourself. "Joe, my son, listen carefully please."

"Yes, Daddy!" Joe said.

"You see and smell all these beautiful flowers in this garden. You can feel the energy of peace eternal here. The human mind, along with the body, must have an energy of peace eternal to have longevity." Dr. Benson continued. "You must eat good foods like fresh green lettuce, spinach, and broccoli raw. This way of eating helps your body be strong and heals any injuries, little Joe!"

Dr. Benson bent down and plucked a piece of dark green lettuce from a vegetable patch, put some in his mouth to eat, and gave some to Joe. They both ate the lettuce while Dr. Benson looked at Joe, and the boy nodded he had understood.

Dr. Benson continued, "Good, Joe! Keep listening. Your mind has something good, not evil, that it wants or desires to accomplish and achieve. This idea in your mind must help you and benefit people." Dr. Benson looked deeply at Joe. "Listen and remember, Joe! All the medicine in the world will not cure or prevent you from getting sick if you do not have peace eternal. Joe, you must search for your peace eternal! I hope you understand me someday, Joe."

"Yes, Daddy! I will search for my peace eternal!" Joe said.

Dr. Benson spotted the rare plant he had discovered with Olivia at John Hughes's greenhouse several years earlier, the one that reacted strangely when he spilled coffee on it. It seemed to resist hot water and cold temperatures, and it changed colors. He thought he would love to add it to his cancer research experiments. He asked Olivia for a piece of it.

"Of course, darling, but on one condition," she said. "Pregnancy makes me famished! May we go eat somewhere?"

Dr. Benson happily agreed, and the three of them drove to a restaurant called La France in Beverly Hills. He ordered escargot, Olivia ordered a blanquette de veau, and Joe got ratatouille. The other diners complimented Joe's outstanding table manners. Music began to play, and soon an opera singer's voice echoed throughout the restaurant. Dr. Benson's skin tingled with excitement while he enjoyed the delicious French food.

"Mrs. Olivia Benson," he said suddenly, "will you honor me with one dance, please, to this exquisite music?"

"It would be my pleasure, Robert, my love!"

They danced together in perfect rhythm while keeping an eye on Joe. When the song ended, they returned to their table. Olivia sipped some water and said, "I don't feel so well. Our baby girl is moving a lot. I think I might actually be having contractions." Dr. Benson checked her pulse and timed two of the contractions. "I knew it," she said. "I'm in labor! Let's go, now!"

Dr. Benson threw three hundred dollars in cash on the table and called, "Keep the change!" He had just enough time to drop a $50 bill in the band's porcelain tip jar before rushing off to the hospital. He called on the way to arrange for triage and a labor and delivery team to be waiting.

At the hospital, the nurse who met them at the entrance said, "Everything is ready, Dr. Benson, but the doctor on call is not available. We do have an experienced, certified nurse-midwife here to help deliver your child."

"I am a physician and a member of the board of this hospital. I will deliver my child with the midwife assisting me."

"Thank you for your help, Dr. Benson. Someone will escort you to the delivery room."

He phoned Adolfo to come and get Joe.

"Don't worry. I happen to be at the bookstore right around the corner!" Adolfo said. "I'll be there in five minutes."

Adolfo arrived quickly. He kissed Olivia on the forehead and said, "My angel, you have the best doctor in the whole world. Don't worry!"

"I know. Thank you, Father!"

"I love you, Mommy," Joe said, kissing her. "I go with Grandfather now. Father, you take care of Mommy, please, please!"

"I will, Joe, don't worry," Dr. Benson assured him. "Go with Grandfather now, okay?"

Adolfo took Joe by the hand and led him from the room. Dr. Benson prepped for the delivery, washing up and putting on latex gloves. The nurse-midwife did the same.

"My name is Maganda," she said. Dr. Benson recognized her accent as Filipino. "It's my pleasure to help such a prestigious physician as you!"

Maganda was an attractive, full-figured woman in her early thirties. She's a former Miss Philippines who exhibited confidence with her every move.

"You don't seem old enough to have so much experience!" Dr. Benson said. "I appreciate your confidence and am grateful for your assistance."

"I have worked as a nurse and midwife for many years. I used to deliver babies in American war zones, and before that I worked for the Red Cross, delivering babies in many countries with other experienced women."

"Very impressive, Maganda! I feel a melding of the minds between us, and I am honored to have you with me."

Maganda blushingly smiled and beamed with confidence. As Dr. Benson smiled back, he saw around her neck a beautiful decorative gold chain, which hung an exquisite handmade gold cross. She noticed him joyfully looking at them and brushed the two slowly with her fingers.

"This gold necklace comes from Manila, and the gold cross belonged to my great grandfather who was a Japanese soldier stationed in Philippines during the World War II. Are they not beautiful? I had them both blessed."

"They are spectacular indeed! And Maganda, since you have them, I see two very beautiful creations from the Philippines, which are extremely blessed!"

The time had come. Dr. Benson and Maganda were ready, and Olivia's feet were up in the stirrups. She held her knees, and at her husband's instruction, she began to push. Thanks to her athleticism and his gentle, loving guidance, the baby soon came wailing into the world.

Olivia immediately brought her daughter to her breast. Dr. Benson kissed his wife and then his daughter.

That night, Olivia and the baby slept peacefully in their private room with a large window overlooking beautiful Beverly Hills. Dr. Benson slipped Maganda one hundred dollars and asked her to buy some fresh pink roses and dark chocolates. She returned with them in the morning, before Olivia was awake.

"Thank you, Maganda," Dr. Benson said. "Please keep the change."

"You are too kind, Dr. Benson. I hope you go to Manila someday and share some of your medical knowledge there. I have a beautiful condo in Manila. I had it built with my overtime money. I would be pleasurably delighted to serve as your personal tour guide in the Philippines if you ever travel there for medical research."

"Why, thank you! Your invitation is both tempting and flattering."

She left the room, smiling with confidence.

Dr. Benson also had confidence now. On the first day of his daughter's life, he was more certain than ever that the cure for cancer was within his grasp. He gazed at his wife and daughter and was overwhelmed with happiness. He had not slept a wink all night, but still felt wide awake.

Olivia's eyes fluttered open. Dr. Benson presented her with the roses and chocolates. "I love you, Olivia. Just look at our beautiful daughter!"

"Thank you, my darling. She is beautiful!"

A pediatrician came to check on the baby, as per hospital procedure. "Thank you, Dr. Benson, for stepping in and assisting us in our time of need," he said. "We are unfortunately short-staffed due to the poor economy."

"It was my pleasure. And by the way, your nurse-midwife Maganda is an excellent professional. You'd better give her a raise, or I'll be tempted to hire her away to form a new research hospital in the Philippines!"

After a final checkup from Olivia's obstetrician, the mother and child were cleared for release. Maganda returned with some final documents for the Bensons to sign.

"And what shall we write down as the name of your beautiful daughter on the birth certificate?" she asked.

Olivia inhaled the scent coming from her roses and kissed their daughter. Then she looked at Dr. Benson and said, "Our daughter is so beautiful and smells so lovely…how about naming her Rose?"

He kissed his tiny girl. "Rose is perfect."

He shared some chocolates with the medical staff, reminding them jokingly that cocoa was a good source of antioxidants. A few of the medical personnel asked shyly if they could have an autograph.

"Sure!" Dr. Benson said. "Can I borrow a pen?"

"Oh, no, sir, thank you. We meant your wife's autograph. She's the famous ballerina!"

Olivia laughed. "Get in line, Dr. Benson!"

He took pictures of her signing autographs. Then they thanked everybody, packed their belongings, and departed the hospital with baby Rose.

Olivia called home on the way. She put the cell phone on speaker so Dr. Benson could hear. "Father, you have a beautiful healthy granddaughter. We are coming home now! How is Joe?"

"Everything's fine. Here's Joe!"

Joe's little voice came through the phone. "Mommy, I miss you. Me and Grandpa are fine. Are you coming home?"

"Yes, sweetheart! Mommy will be home soon, and we have a surprise for you."

They heard Joe laughing and wended their way back to their mansion in Beverly Hills.

11

"It feels good to be home," Olivia said as they pulled up their driveway to park. Her eyes lit up. "Look, Rose, there's Mommy's garden!"

Adolfo and Joe greeted them at the door. Olivia took the baby to the bedroom to nurse, while Dr. Benson went to the kitchen to make brunch for the family.

Soon Olivia came downstairs. "Rose is fast asleep in her crib," she said, joining Joe, Adolfo, and her husband at the dining table.

Adolfo did not touch his breakfast, saying, "No, thank you, I already had my breakfast drink." He then departed to exercise in the gym room.

Joe nibbled a little of his eggs and hot dogs, then spit them out and said, "No more eggs! No more hot dogs!" He ate a piece of fruit from a bowl in the center of the table instead and washed it down with huge gulps of water.

"Robert, how many times have you cooked eggs or hot dogs in your life?" she asked.

"Quite possibly never," he admitted. "I'm sorry, honey. I looked the recipes up in a cookbook, though. Didn't they work?"

"Oh, sweetheart, can't you tell? They're burned to a crisp!"

"Time is precious to me!" he said defensively. "Someone else has always cooked for me, or I've just eaten raw fruit and vegetables. That allows me more time for research. I suppose now that I am a father and husband, I should learn more about doing work in the household."

"Darling, you know I made plenty of money as a ballet dancer, and you receive so many donations from wealthy patients, Hollywood actors, famous entertainers, and political leaders. Surely we can afford a chef and a housekeeper. Just no gardener, please! I prefer to do it myself. And besides, my father helps me."

Adolfo, my clever father-in-law, Dr. Benson thought. He has devised a way to be close not only to his daughter and grandchildren, but to his doctor as well.

"I think it's a great idea," he said. "And your father can also help protect the family while I am busy with research."

—⚶—

Several chefs were interviewed for the job. They settled on a French chef called Napoleon who had a pleasant personality and an impressive résumé. He could prepare food from all over the world—France, England, Italy, Spain, Saudi Arabia, China, Japan, and America. He was especially skilled at preparing fruits de mer, or seafood platter, which was Dr. Benson's favorite.

Napoleon had attended culinary school in Europe and the United States. His father, a French ambassador and a world-class fencing instructor, also taught fencing to his son, who went on to win a silver medal at the Olympics before turning to cooking. Napoleon's mother was a schoolteacher in France and had taught him proper mealtime manners from a very young age. Many French believe young children are born in a state of ignorance, not innocence, and therefore must be given correct values and discipline from early childhood. Napoleon, an only child, was able to tour many different countries when he was growing up. This helped him become familiar with many different kinds of cuisine. He said that he had always felt a void in his life, not having a brother or sister to play with, so he poured his loneliness and concentration into cooking and fencing.

Dr. Benson and Olivia both voted for Napoleon as chef but also wanted him to receive little Joe's approval. Napoleon whipped up some crêpes stuffed with fluffy eggs and creamy cheese. He winked at Joe, puckered up, and gave his lips a quick slap with his fingers, making a loud pop. Joe giggled as Napoleon placed the food in front of him.

"Eggs, Joe, eggs!" Herbie squawked.

Little Joe wrinkled his nose. Dr. Benson knew he was remembering the eggs his daddy burned. Joe took a little taste and then began to eat faster and faster, as if he could not get enough of them.

"Honey, slow down!" Olivia said, laughing. Joe put down his fork and drank some water.

"I guess that settles it!" said Dr. Benson as he signed Napoleon's contract. "My clever wife keeps a garden full of vegetables and fruits, and there is a freshwater well. Please use whatever you like."

Napoleon's eyes flickered with excitement. "A chef's dream!" He made the popping sound again by slapping his hand against his puckered mouth.

The next task was to hire a housekeeper. They interviewed many interesting candidates. The final woman to be interviewed was a beautiful young lady named Lumbra. The Bensons were a little tired by the time they interviewed her, but they decided to meet with her because they were eager to hire a good worker who would benefit all of them. Lumbra had a bright smile, gorgeous face, and curvy body.

"Hola, how are you?" she said.

"Please sit down, Lumbra," Olivia said. Lumbra sat down and crossed her long, supple-looking legs. She spoke with an attractive Spanish accent. She explained that she spoke fluent Spanish and English. She had been born and raised in Mexico City when her father, an archaeologist, took a job there. Because he had been born in Corpus Christi, Texas, Lumbra was able to claim American citizenship while she was a minor, with help from an immigration attorney friend of her father's. She now had dual citizenship. She told them that her father had bought them a large hacienda in Mexico to live in while he traveled to conduct archaeological expeditions throughout the world. Many times, she and her mother would go with him to be together as a family, unless the trip was dangerous.

"Ms. Lumbra, your father sounds like he was great at keeping the family together most of the time," Dr. Benson said. "Tell us, what is a hacienda?"

"It's like a large mansion that's outside of the city. It's like a ranch, where you can have horses and goats."

"Oh, now we get the picture. That must have been a nice way to live."

"Well, nice in a way, but keeping a hacienda clean is a lot of work when you have no servants."

Olivia raised an eyebrow. "Then you know how I feel keeping this whole mansion running with hardly any help!"

Dr. Benson laughed because he knew that the comment was directed at him.

"Mama and I decided to not have any servants, so we learned how to clean a huge place efficiently. That way, Father could have more money to use to expand his archaeological expeditions."

"You're so well-traveled," Dr. Benson said. "Why do you wish to be a housekeeper?"

"I want to live in a big place like this mansion, which I am accustomed to, and I want to attend college nearby to study archaeology so I can be an archeologist like my father. I need the money for school. I loved how my father took us on so many expeditions, but he did not have good medical coverage. He died in an accident on an archaeology expedition in Patmos. My mother was so sad that she fell ill and died soon after, because we did not have good medical coverage. After that, there was no money left and no one had money to pay a fair price for the hacienda. So I locked it up and went to Los Angeles to live with my aunt, who had moved there from Corpus Christi. I'm living with her still, but I don't want to be a burden."

"Ms. Lumbra, an old scientist friend contacted me to give you a good reference. He says he knows you, and that he knew your father," said Dr. Benson.

"How nice. My father left me very little money, but he had many educated friends around the world!"

"How do we know you are good with children?" Olivia asked. "You are very attractive. Don't you have any boyfriends?"

"My father told me to choose one goal and make it the most important thing in my life. And my goal, Mrs. Benson, is to become an archaeologist. Once I become an archaeologist, I will pursue two missions. First, complete the search of my father's last archaeological expedition site on the island of Patmos. Second, search the Mayan and Aztec pyramids for two books my father wrote about, the Book of Kukulcan and Book of Itzamna. My father's notes say that a possibly celestial being called Saman had the sole access to these two books. If someday I fall in love and get married, it will be to someone who loves me deeply, and is willing to travel with me throughout the world on archaeological expeditions with our children—as I once did with my father and mother."

At that moment, Joe walked in and sat right next to Lumbra, smiling at her like an infatuated puppy. Olivia and Dr. Benson looked at each other and said, "Okay, we know Joe likes you, and it seems he likes you a lot! Ms. Lumbra, would you excuse us a moment, please? We will return with our decision."

Lumbra nodded and struck up a conversation with Joe. The Bensons asked Napoleon to keep an eye on her and Joe while they talked.

"Yes, madame!" he said and made his popping sound by striking his mouth with his hand. They stepped into the next room.

"She is very beautiful," Olivia said. "How can I trust her around you alone?"

"I love you, Olivia! Lumbra will be fine. Her father was a very intelligent man, one of my colleague's friends. Besides, she will be totally concentrated on looking after our house and on her college studies. The bonus is that Joe likes her. You know he does not trust everybody. As for me, I am too busy with my research to pay Lumbra any attention. All my time is spent in the laboratory or with you!"

"Fine, Robert, let's hire her on a trial basis first, to observe how everything works out."

They agreed on a one-month trial. Back in the living room, Lumbra, Joe, and Napoleon were eating hors d'oeuvres and laughing. The Bensons told Lumbra that she was hired as a live-in housekeeper who would also serve as a babysitter when Olivia was out rehearsing or performing.

"Oh, thank you!" she said. "You will like me, I know it. I feel honored to be in this house with you!"

At that moment, Herbie flew into the room, looking for Joe, and squawked, "Honor in this house!" Then he whistled.

Napoleon escorted Lumbra out of the mansion so that she could retrieve her belongings from her aunt's house and come to live with the happy and lucky Benson family.

12

Everything seemed to be going fine with the full-time chef and full-time housekeeper. Dr. Benson had more time to concentrate on his research goal, and his enthusiasm had never been higher. He was experimenting on a piece of Olivia's chameleon-like plant. He took an extract from it and added the formula he was using on his research volunteer patients from the barrio. He focused on human subjects so that he could cut to the chase and see how human cancers responded to his medication.

It was time for him to visit Roger, the veteran, and Pete, the homeless man with liver cancer. He started up his powerful SLS AMG supercar Mercedes-Benz and tore off like a dragster out of the driveway. He went to their sleazy hotel with money, food, and some clothes.

"I was wondering when you were going to show up!" Roger said.

"Don't worry, I am your personal doctor," Dr. Benson said while he administered the new medication. Pete went to sleep right after receiving his dose. Dr. Benson promised to check on them again in a week.

The day before he was to see them again, Roger left him a message on his cell phone, saying his friend Pete had seemed cured, but then his jaundice eyes returned as if he had cancer again. Dr. Benson decided to finish some family business and then visit Roger and Pete. He felt thankful yet again for the blessing of having a full-time chef and housekeeper so that he and Olivia could pursue their professional goals.

—m—

General Arnold Benson also arrived on leave that day to stay with the Bensons for a while. Lumbra prepared the guest room for him with fresh sheets, bath towels, shampoo, and soap. The whole family ate in the formal dining room.

"We have soufflés today!" said Napoleon. He had also prepared various vegetables, fresh fruits, salads, grains, and Japanese nattō (fermented soybeans). Beverages on offer included water, freshly squeezed fruit juices, and freshly ground hot coffee. As they ate, each adult strove to teach Joe and Rose good manners. They corrected their eating techniques, taught them conversational skills, and encouraged them to be good listeners. The Bensons expected honor and respect from everyone at the dining table and encouraged each person to feel free to speak whatever was on his or her mind.

After dining, General Benson and his son went to the study to talk privately. The general puffed on a nice Honduran cigar as they talked. Dr. Benson showed him a sample living trust that had been prepared by the family attorney, Basil Hermes. It stated that if anything should happen to Olivia or Dr. Benson, the general was to become a successor trustee, full guardian of the children, with authority over their bank trust account as well. It also included a document that outlined what they wanted for their upbringing. Dr. Benson had always believed that a person's mind brought out the fruit of their spirit, and that the young mind must be educated early so it would open up to creative ideas and consequently would help mankind. The document included their preferences for the children's religion and specified that Rose should study piano, music composition, and voice, and that Joe should be instructed in swordsmanship and martial arts of all kinds.

Mr. Hermes arrived soon afterward with the official final documents. He was an intelligent and feared attorney-at-law, a powerful-looking Greek man in his early fifties. Just as he was presenting the documents for Dr. Benson and the general to sign, however, there was a knock at the door.

"Gentlemen, may I come in?" Olivia asked.

"Of course, honey. Please come in and have a seat, I was just going to get you." Dr. Benson said.

Olivia sat down in a fine oak chair to listen to the attorney.

"Mrs. Olivia and Dr. Robert Benson, you both are doing well by having this living trust implemented," Mr. Hermes said. "A living trust prevents the state from conducting a formal, expensive probate, which would benefit the state's interests and not your children, Joe and Rose. Please review all the documents carefully and please let me know if you both have any questions."

Olivia and her husband, along with General Benson, reviewed the documents. Then they all happily signed the papers.

Olivia kissed her father-in-law on the cheek as she said, "Thank you for honoring us by agreeing to be the guardian of our children and agreeing to our terms. We're off to bed. Good night, my favorite honorable general!"

"Good night, my angel of a daughter-in-law. Guten abend, Robert, my boy!"

"Guten nacht, Father," Robert said. And Dr. Benson then turns to his guest, "Good night, Basil, old friend!"

Mr. Basil Hermes only smiled back. He'd never been much for words. Dr. Benson couldn't help but notice that the attorney was wearing a Water Mason ring just like his father's. General Benson and Mr. Hermes remained in the study to go over a few final details regarding the living trust. Dr. Benson could smell his father's Honduran cigar as he and Olivia made their way upstairs.

—m—

Dr. Benson was awakened in the middle of the night by the ring of his cell phone. It was Roger. He said something was not right. Dr. Benson got in his supercar and sped to the motel to see how his patients were doing. He found a lot of candy wrappers outside their door. No one answered his knock, so he used his key card to enter. There were more candy wrappers on the floor inside, along with empty liquor bottles and donut boxes.

"Roger? Pete? Are you here?"

Dr. Benson noticed a stench in the air and covered his mouth and nose with his hand. Then he spotted Roger and Pete lying on the floor. They both smelled bad from poor hygiene. Both weren't moving. Roger was covered with candy wrappers, Pete with liquor bottles. Dr. Benson put on latex gloves and checked their vital signs, but it was as he feared—they were both dead. He suspected that all the sugar they had consumed paralyzed most of their white blood cells. Their terrible diet and lack of exercise were just too much for his special medication to overcome.

He wondered why they had not followed the regimen, and why they worried about things like food when he was providing for them. Did their minds have peace eternal? Cancer was not a contagious disease, but for it to be cured, he knew that the mind must be at peace and not abused by consumption of bad toxins.

He slipped out into the parking lot, relieved that the cheap motel had no security cameras.

"Good-bye, Roger. Good-bye, Pete," he murmured. "I'm so sorry I couldn't help you. Thank you for your efforts."

Dr. Benson felt remorse as he cried aloud, "I will send money to their next of kin, and pay separately for their burials." Dr. Benson used his hands-free, high-tech cell phone to contact a mortician friend. He asked him to pick up the bodies.

As he flew back down the road to the Beatles's song "Let It Be," he thought about his mother, Mary. He had promised her that he would find a cure for cancer, and all diseases that plagued mankind. Now he would have to find more human medical research volunteer subjects; he knew there was a risk to them, but, he reasoned, benefitting the many outweighed the risk of injuring a few.

Out of nowhere, a police car appeared behind him and seemed to follow the Mercedes.

"Damn!" Dr. Benson said. "When you need those guys, you can't find them, and when you don't want to see them, there they are!"

He wondered if someone had found Roger and Pete's dead bodies, or had seen him leaving the hotel. The sun hadn't come up yet, but the street lamps were still on. It was half past three in the morning. Dr. Benson was tired. No one was walking the streets, and no one was on the roads except Dr. Benson and the cop. Dr. Benson had been too busy with his medical research these days, consequently he had not washed off the pigeon crap that covered his entire car license plate letters and numbers. Could this be the reason a police car appeared behind him? He was worried. The police car lights begin to flash.

Then the policeman called out over his loudspeaker, "Pull your car over and stop your vehicle!"

Dr. Benson wondered if he might be able to outrun the cop. There was no one else on the road to get in his way. Or should he just stop there, allow himself to be arrested, and end his tiresome pursuit of finding a cure for cancer? Roger and Pete had signed a medical research volunteer release form, but if this cop was pulling him over in conjunction with their deaths, he was not going to be interested in hearing about that at three thirty in the morning. He cranked up "Let It Be" loud enough to drown out the police siren and flicked the metal switch to activate his custom rear spoiler. It was made by the Saman Corporation and had an advanced computer-chip brain that allowed it to move, giving the vehicle enhanced aerodynamic mobility around corners and reducing the car's lift when it was traveling fast. Dr. Benson had a lead foot and put the German supercar into high gear.

A smile of tolerance came across Dr. Benson's face. He knew if he eluded this cop that was nobly trying to do his duty, he would still have a shot at finding a cure for cancer. As he listened to "Let It Be" on his crisp-sounding speakers, he knew that was what mattered most. He sped down the road as his spoiler fin adjusted when he went around corners; the car hugged them, smooth and tight. He felt grateful for the supercar. He reminisced as he drove about the time when some of his mother's German relatives taught him how to drive fast in Germany, allowing him to practice with their race cars on real racetracks. After that, the German autobahns seemed like a breeze. *Maybe someday I will have my own race car*, he mused. But first things first: he must still fulfill his promise to his mother.

The police officer fruitlessly did his best to keep up as they flew around turns. Dr. Benson heard a helicopter and knew it was probably in pursuit of him as well, but between the powerful engine and his skillful driving, he was able to elude both. He breathed a sigh of relief as he arrived home safely.

"I believe everything happens for a reason," he said to himself.

13

Several more years passed, and Joe and Rose continued to grow up. Dr. Benson continued to conduct his research. Though he had not yet succeeded in finding a cure for cancer, he recognized his defeats as learning opportunities, not as complete failures. If it took his whole lifetime to find the cure, so be it.

One day, Dr. Benson's mind felt tired, so he lay down on his bed and inclined his forehead so it was hanging off the edge, with his face facing down. This allowed maximum blood flow to his brain, helping to nourish his mind.

Joe happened to walk in and ask, "What are you doing, Daddy?"

"Well, son, I'm giving energy and health to my brain. Come join Daddy, Joe!"

"Yes, Daddy! Mommy is trying to teach Rose how to dance ballet, but Rose keeps falling down. She is an awful dancer, Daddy! I don't think Rose likes ballet."

Dr. Benson laughed while Joe mimicked his father by lying down in the same way.

"Joe, there are two ways to do this," Dr. Benson said. "The way we are doing it is the easy way. And the hard way is facing the ceiling while your forehead is off the edge of the bed. You have to be an athlete like your mother to do it the hard way."

Once Joe heard that, he rolled over to face the ceiling while his forehead remained inclined down toward the floor.

"Amazing! I believe we have another athlete in the family." Dr. Benson beamed with pride.

—⁕—

One day, a patient named Mr. Musashi came to the Bensons' house to personally thank the doctor for curing him of his Parkinson's, Alzheimer's, and arthritis.

"Okay, Mr. Musashi. I need to examine you, my friend. Please take off your shirt and lay on this medical bed that has a new machine I received free from the Saman Corporation." Dr. Benson says.

"Hai. Yes!" Mr. Musashi says. As Dr. Benson smiles to use his new computer, he hooks up its echocardiogram to record the heart rate and the electroencephalography to record the brain waves.

"Mr. Musashi, please speak so your voice is also recorded to see any patterns of speech that I could use later for health reasons."

Mr. Musashi speaks and starts speaking with Joe, who came to watch his father in admiration. Dr. Benson's Saman Corporation computer glows red as it records Mr. Musashi's voice, mannerism, heart function, and brain waves. "Mr. Musashi is not only my patient, but he is my friend, Joe," Dr. Benson says. Mr. Musashi put's his shirt back on as Dr. Benson completes his examination. "Looking good, Mr. Musashi. Keep it up!"

Joe, who was now seven years old, really hit it off with Mr. Musashi.

"Please take these three plane tickets Dr. Benson for you and your family!" Mr. Musashi says as he smiles at Joe. However, Dr. Benson respectfully declined his offer of free plane tickets so the family could visit Mr. Musashi in Japan, but he struck another deal: Mr. Musashi would teach Joe the art of being a samurai warrior. The Musashi family knew its true secrets and could impart their philosophy to others. Dr. Benson knew that Joe's idol was Robin Hood, and he believed it would be a good idea for Joe to learn discipline and concentration when handling a sword. Learning

Bushidō—the way of the warrior knight—would help Joe to overcome many of life's adversities.

"I can't thank you enough for curing me," Mr. Musashi said. "I would be pleased to pay back this honor with a deed of my own. I will teach Joe everything I know about Bushidō so that your bloodline will have great longevity. Joe will one day be a great, benevolent samurai!"

Dr. Benson spent quality time with Joe when he could, but he realized he also spent an enormous amount of time in the laboratory. He felt happy, therefore, knowing he found a good coach in Mr. Musashi. He would assist Joe in his personal search for his peace eternal.

Dr. Benson smiled. "What do you think of Mr. Musashi's offer, Joe?"

"Wow, Dad! Imagine, I could be Robin Hood and a samurai! Thank you, Father."

Mr. Musashi informed them that he often flew back and forth from Japan to Los Angeles on business trips, so he would be able to come to Beverly Hills to teach Joe once a week. This worked well for Dr. Benson too, since he could also use the visits to check on the health of his patient.

Sensei Musashi gave Joe a wooden sword and showed him how to grip it properly.

"Joe, since you are right-handed, place your right hand one finger-width from the tsuba, or sword guard. Grip the sword with one or two hands, but with the palm supporting the sword. Always grip the sword from the top, not the sides, and never place your thumbs on top." Sensei Musashi inserted Joe's sheathed sword into his belt. "How does that feel, Joe?"

"It feels fine, Sensei, thank you," Joe said.

"Stand up straight. No slumping, Joe. Fill yourself with pride and remember that when a samurai stands, sits, or walks, he shows honor. He is proud. You will learn to honor your teacher, honor yourself, and honor your sword. Joe, you will learn the art of rei!" Sensei Musashi said. The lessons for Joe are authentic Bushido, which gave ancient samurais success.

Before Sensei Musashi left, he taught Joe the etiquette of bowing to one's sensei and bowing to the sword. He showed him how important body language and eye contact were. He also said that for lesson two, Joe would be instructed how to wear an obi and traditional hakama pants.

"Joe, you will also learn the Japanese language, so you will be a true samurai!" Sensei Musashi proclaimed.

Joe bowed formally. "Sayonara. Good-bye Sensei!"

"Sayonara, then, Joe," Mr. Musashi said. "I will return soon."

—◊—

Everything happens for a reason, Dr. Benson thought to himself. He and Joe went to watch Olivia give five-year-old Rose a piano lesson. It was too bad Rose did not enjoy learning ballet; she also wasn't athletic. However, she did extremely enjoy the piano lessons her mother gave her.

Olivia said to her daughter, "Rose, use charming concentration. Remember that they will all come to hear and see you play. You, Rose, are the star. Attract them with the way you smile, the way you touch the piano keys, and the way you sing. Connect your heart with their hearts! Also, honey, remember these keys A through G, for these will always be your friends, and never let you down." Rose thought she needed friends, especially friends that would never let you down.

Olivia continued to teach Rose everything she knew about—how to be a star entertainer.

"Yes, Mommy, use my heart!" Rose said.

They started to sing, and Dr. Benson thought that Rose sounded like a little songbird. Just then, Herbie made one of his signature flights into the room, seemingly from nowhere, and landed softly on the piano, close to Rose. While Rose played, the parrot danced left and right, picking up the beat.

The pleasant smell of flowers entered through an open window. Dr. Benson looked out the window to the garden and saw Adolfo working there. Olivia's garden was a pleasure to the eyes, and it brought calmness and happiness to all the senses. The house was sparkling clean thanks to Lumbra, and there was healthy food available at every hour thanks to Napoleon. Dr. Benson recognized that this was truly a quality moment to remember.

—⚬⚬—

Several months went by, during which Joe received many constructive and fun lessons with his katana sword, including suemonogiri (cutting tatami mats). Sensei Musashi enjoyed teaching this skill in particular to his student. Two wet rice straw mats were rolled up and placed, standing vertically, on separate stands two feet apart. Joe focused with kime. In his mind, they simulated two opponents. Joe used both hands for more control while he swung his katana sword at them several times, using his hip and back shoulder blade muscles to generate energy for power.

"Kia!" Joe shouted as his katana sword broke wind through the air, and he cut the two rice mats into seven pieces as they softly fell to the floor. Joe had done an unbelievable feat for his young age; however, Sensei Musashi always searched for more improvement.

"Good, Joe, yet to become samurai one day you will accomplish this feat while using only the right or left hand!" Sensei Musashi proclaimed.

Joe told his family that he was beginning to learn to use a sword properly. According to Sensei, he was learning many wise philosophies that taught warriors the meaning of life as well.

One day, the family gathered in the gym, where Olivia had recently placed a small upright piano and one guitar. She had felt to encourage her son, Joe, into the music world, but Joe seems only interested in swordplay. However, she did manage to teach her husband a few light piano tunes, which somehow he enjoyed. The very observant Olivia had kept abreast of matters and noticed General Benson had challenged Joe to a duel in swordplay.

Olivia's beautiful garden was visible through the huge gym window. It gave the room a comfortable, open feel, not that anyone in the Benson family was claustrophobic. Dr. Benson had brought a bowl of mixed nuts for them to munch on—sunflower seeds, flax seeds, peanuts, almonds, cashews, and walnuts. All were a great source of lignans, chemical compounds that are estrogenic. In humans, Dr. Benson knew, high levels of lignans correlated to lower stress levels and peace of mind. People who had plenty were less likely succumb to cancer. Dr. Benson was trying to teach his children that it was better to snack on nuts and seeds than to eat candy. The family sat patiently, waiting for the event to begin. Joe and Grandpa Benson suited up in their kendo outfits and gear.

"Father, put some music on, please!" Joe called.

Dr. Benson picked up a remote. They had speakers networked in every room of the house. "What kind of music, son?"

"Your favorite and mine, Joaquín Rodrigo!"

Dr. Benson activated the music.

Adolfo came in to join them. "Whip his bloody pants off, little Joe!"

The general shrugged. "Engländer dummkopf! I guess my grandson has the home-field advantage."

Slighted, Adolfo says, "Hey! Be careful! I know a little kraut too."

"En garde, Grandfather!" Joe shouted. "Welcome to Sherwood!"

"Ha ha," said General Benson, playing along. "I am the sheriff of Nottingham! Give me all your money and those pretty shoes too."

Joe looked down at his feet. "What pretty shoes?"

At that moment, General Benson lunged and scored a point on Joe.

"That was dishonest, Grandfather!" Joe complained.

"Yes, it was. But you must learn the art of complete concentration, as I did at West Point. Remember this, people are dishonest and will trick you and lie to you. They will try to make you fail. You must not let them!"

Joe listened respectfully. He remembered something Sensei Musashi had said: "When you make a mistake, ask yourself what lesson you can learn. This is the way!"

Joe closed his eyes and felt the music with his spirit. Then he reopened his eyes slowly, using a Japanese samurai skill called metsuke—making eye contact with spiritual intent. Music was a good training aid that Sensei Musashi had taught Joe to use to develop enhanced metsuke. Joe gracefully sidestepped his grandfather's attacks by sensing his energy and countered quickly, scoring numerous points. He continued to move, slash, and thrust when openings presented themselves.

Dr. Benson, Olivia, and Rose snacked on the nuts as they watched the entertainment. At one point, Dr. Benson reached into the bowl at the same moment as Olivia.

"These are good, Robert," she said.

"These are good, Robert," said another, higher-pitched voice.

It didn't belong to Rose. Dr. Benson suddenly saw Herbie with his beak in the bowl.

"Ooh! Ooh!" the bird squawked before flying into Rose's arms for protection. Dr. Benson turned his attention back to the duel. Dr. Benson used infinite intelligence as he walked over to the piano and sat down. He had his mind drift off into intuitive thought processes while he strummed the piano keys to light musical tunes.

"My arm is hurt, Joe," General Benson said. "Please come here and help me!"

Joe hesitated, but eventually let his guard down and came forward to help his grandfather. General Benson immediately grabbed him.

"You fell for a military tactic, little Joe. Many a war's been won by luring the enemy out from behind its battlements then launching an all-out attack!" General Benson proclaimed.

At that moment, Dr. Benson got up from the piano, saying, "There, now I've got it!" Joe, a little confused about what happened since he thought swordplay was fair play.

"I thought you might be tricking me, Grandfather!" Joe said.

"Yes, that's right. Your gut instinct told you it was a trick, but you refused to believe it!"

"But how do you know when your gut instinct is right?" Joe asked, confused.

"Your gut instinct is always right, but you must practice listening to it so you learn to trust it. Then you will never doubt it. I have one final thing to say to you today. Everyone has a purpose and a mission in life. As you learn to use your mind and trust your instinct, you too will find your purpose and mission in life."

"Your grandfather is right," Dr. Benson said. "And thank you, Father, for teaching our son about honesty and purpose. And your lesson on military tactics gave me an idea about the possible missing key strategy to remedy diseases. I will implement your military strategy to find a cure. I must!" Dr. Benson looks up to the sky. "I love you, Mom. I'm almost there!"

Joe and his grandfather shook hands. Dr. Benson also jubilantly shook his father's hand. Joe clearly admired his grandfather.

"I hope I go to West Point someday to learn all the great things benevolent leaders should know, like you did," he said.

"We will see which path is yours to take, little Joe. If you are to be a leader, then your future is definitely at West Point. If you're to be an inventor, then you must go to an engineering institute. If you decide to pursue medicine like your father, then you must find the best medical school. And let's not forget, men of the cloth give the world honor too! Someday God will speak to you, Joe, and then you will know your destiny."

"Thank you, Grandfather. I look forward to that day. Good night!"

"Good night, Joe. Mein enkelkind."

Dr. Benson took his son upstairs to bed. Before Joe went to sleep, they read a story about a Japanese warrior who asked for God's help in combating an evil villain. Because the warrior knew God was with him, he defeated the villain. Joe enjoyed the story and fell fast asleep as soon as it ended. Meanwhile, Olivia played some music on the small piano in Rose's room until she fell asleep too.

Dr. Benson and Olivia took a walk in the garden together, holding hands.

"Robert, I wish we could live forever!" she said in her beautiful English accent.

"Olivia, my love! Think of all the good things in life that are under your control, and enjoy them in the now."

He embraced her and told her how much he loved her. They kissed passionately.

At that romantic moment, Dr. Benson saw Herbie in his peripheral vision. The parrot had been flying around the garden, but suddenly he flew up through the open window of their bedroom.

Probably to be with the children, Dr. Benson thought. *He's better than a watchdog! He watched everybody and everything all the time.*

"What are you thinking?" Olivia asked.

"Oh, just about Herbie, our watch parrot. And how much I love you and the children! But…"

"I know, my dear. You can't be satisfied until you've found your cure. I know you miss your mother, but don't forget that you still have your father and your wife and children. You will succeed one day. I know you will."

14

A few intense, tiresome weeks passed as Dr. Benson conducted round-the-clock experiments at the Beverly Hills Research Hospital. He had been using compound inhibitors to flush out hidden diseases from reservoir-infected DNA cells. Then he injected them simultaneously with a formula that he had developed; the treatment attacked disease and rendered it unable to escape from a cell. The ambush tactic had been inspired by the general. Rumors had spread fast and far among the elite that Dr. Benson had found a cure for HIV and AIDS. He scheduled a press conference about his new treatment.

One day, the king of Saudi Arabia came to visit the hospital because his son and heir, Prince Aadil, had been cured by Dr. Benson. The prince had contracted HIV through a blood transfusion a few years earlier. But now, thanks to Dr. Benson, he was disease-free. The wise King Mohammed and his beautiful wife,

Queen Rima, entered their son's room. Dr. Benson was there, checking on his patient.

Tears streamed down the king and queen's faces as they hugged their son, saying, "Shukran Allah! Shukran, Dr. Benson! Thank you!"

"You are most welcome," Dr. Benson said.

"May I shake your hand for saving my son and my bloodline?" the king asked. They shook hands while Queen Rima knelt at her son's bedside, weeping with gratitude. "Do you have a son?"

"Yes, his name is Joe."

"Allah has truly blessed you, Doctor. You have a boy to carry on your legacy."

"I also have a musically talented daughter to sing my legacy," said Dr. Benson with a laugh.

"Indeed! Please allow me to offer you some wisdom that was handed down to me from my father's fathers. Because of what you have done, Doctor, you are with Allah. But evil sees this and may try to strike you down. I will send some of my personal guards to watch over you while you give your press conference."

"You are very kind, Your Highness, but that's not necessary," Dr. Benson said. "I know God has chosen a path for me, and he will protect me."

The king and queen kissed his hand.

Prince Aadil said, "I will always be indebted to you and your family. If one day Allah gives me the opportunity to save your life or the life of someone in your family, I will."

Not only was the press conference a success, Dr. Benson learned soon after it that he was to be awarded a Nobel Prize for his work. This was the second time he had received the honor; the first time was for his development of cures for Alzheimer's, arthritis, and Parkinson's. He prepared a speech to give before the many scientists, politicians, and others who would be assembled to honor him.

"Ladies and gentlemen," he said at the awards ceremony. "I feel grateful to be here today in the presence of all you fine human beings, and in the presence of God. Once again, for the second time, I feel honored to receive this prize. I thank you all. I know the human race is fortunate that I discovered a cure for AIDS, and I hope that the world will be a happier place because of it. In honesty, I never set out to discover a cure for AIDS, but I am grateful that this deadly virus no longer plagues mankind.

"My original plan was always to find a cure for cancer; this is still my burning desire. I am pleased to tell you that I am close. At this moment, my medication can only put cancer into remission, it always returns eventually. But I am determined. I have eliminated all unnecessary distractions from my life and work so that I might devote all my concentration to finding a cure.

"Ladies and gentlemen, my final message is this. When we use our infinite intelligence, imagination, and creativity, nothing is impossible. Thank you, God bless you, and good-bye, my fellow honorable human beings!"

15

Dr. Benson was performing a full-body CT scan on Adolfo for an overall health review. As he looked over the results, he drank a cup of joe for energy. The scan revealed that Adolfo had a tumor in his abdomen. Dr. Benson immediately started high-intensity ultrasound treatment directly on the tumor, in hopes that it would be neutralized and Adolfo might not need chemotherapy. Dr. Benson did not like using chemotherapy unless absolutely necessary since it killed beneficial white blood cells along with cancer cells.

Dr. Benson convinced his father-in-law to come and live with them so he could enjoy his last days with his daughter and grandchildren. Since Adolfo's health was declining, Dr. Benson offered him his new cancer medication, with the warning that it had not been proven safe for humans. Dr. Benson was always continuing to work on his cancer medication, updating it. He believed the current version was special.

"Please let me try it," Adolfo said. "I love my daughter and I want to see my grandchildren grow up."

"If you wish to try it, I will give it to you." Dr. Benson said. "First, I will surgically remove the tumor in your stomach. You will not need chemotherapy because the high-intensity ultrasound has neutralized the tumor and stopped the metastatic cancer seed cells from being released. Then I will administer my new medication, which has a combination of supercharged granulocytes and an enzyme from a rare plant that's been growing in Olivia's garden. This rare plant is the same plant we had brought from John Hughes's greenhouse."

"Please tell me more about this plant!"

"It probably dates back to the time of Noah. I came to this conclusion through my own research, and because of some notes I found from Sir Isaac Newton's last days. He researched the Scriptures and wrote what he discovered in a code that I deciphered. Man was created from the earth, and his blood contains the same percentage of salt as ocean water does. The answer has been right in front of us the whole time. Living plants grow in soil, the purest form of earth, and when ingested, give longevity. So I asked myself, when did human beings live a very long time? The Bible tells us that Noah lived to be 950 years old, so perhaps a plant from his time was the key. I remembered the ancient plant in Olivia's garden and wondered if it could be the link to the missing enzyme I have been looking for. Now, Adolfo, it is crucial that after I administer all these medications you follow the entire regimen that comes along with them."

"I agree to everything, Robert."

—⁓—

Olivia still did not know that her father was dying of cancer, so Dr. Benson told her that he merely wanted Adolfo to stay with them temporarily so that he could monitor his blood chemistry and exercise routine. She agreed and instructed Lumbra to get a room ready on the other side of their manor house, near the gym, so that Adolfo would have quick and easy access to exercise and her family would still have some privacy. Dr. Benson gave Napoleon a list of foods that Adolfo was allowed to eat: raw nuts, nattō beans, eggplant, raw fruits and vegetables, and wheatgrass. He was not to have any white sugars, refined flours, alcohol, or tobacco, and very little cooked food. He needed to have plenty of water, freshly squeezed fruit juices, and vegetables prepared fresh from the garden every day.

After Napoleon looked over the list, he said, "Oui, monsieur!" and made his trademark popping sound by slapping his fingers over his puckered mouth.

"Ha! Ha! Thank you, Napoleon."

Dr. Benson drew up a mandatory exercise regimen for Adolfo, which he planned to monitor via the gym's surveillance camera. Adolfo knew Dr. Benson would be watching him. Dr. Benson had to be sure Adolfo would follow his diet and exercise program to the letter while he took the new cancer medication.

16

After several months of treatment, Adolfo became the very picture of health. Dr. Benson ran a new CT scan. The results showed no cancer or suspicious nodules. Next, Dr. Benson checked Adolfo's blood by conducting a circulating tumor cell test, where a genetic analysis could identify the expression of therapeutic targets and of chemo-resistance markers unique to Adolfo's circulating tumor cells. The test showed no potential metastatic cancer cells.

Dr. Benson ran from his basement laboratory to the kitchen when he was finished reviewing the results and said, "Napoleon, fresh cup of joe please!"

"Oui, oui, monsieur!"

Moments later, the coffee was ready.

"Thanks," Dr. Benson said. "I need some energetic alkaline in my blood!"

He took one…two…three sips. A calming effect came over him. He went into the study and continued drinking his cup of joe.

Napoleon brought in a hot pot of coffee, set it on the table. "Au revoir, docteur!" he said, making a double pop noise by way of farewell.

Dr. Benson sat alone, drinking coffee and listening to "Let It Be." Memories of his mother, Mary, flooded his mind. He tried to control his emotions, but tears started falling into his coffee cup. Suddenly he had a clear vision of his mother in heaven saying, "Robert, you can rest now. Your life is complete. We will be together soon!"

Dr. Benson stood up. "Adolfo," he called through the house's intercom system. "Come to my study, please!"

A few minutes later, Adolfo appeared in his exercise clothes. Dr. Benson offered him a chair and a cup of joe, and then shared the good news.

"Your test results are in. You are completely cured of all cancer."

Adolfo dropped his cup on the floor, rose from his seat, and grabbed Dr. Benson's hand.

"Thank you, Robert. Thank you, God!" he exclaimed tearfully, hugging his son-in-law. Then stood still as a tree and said, "Excuse me, please. I have to go see my grandchildren and my daughter!" He ran joyfully out of the room.

Dr. Benson sat and savored his cup of joe and the incredible moment.

I, Dr. Benson, have finally discovered the cure for cancer, he thought. My life's work is complete.

—⟋⟍—

Dr. Benson awoke the next day to a beautiful morning. He smiled because he knew that, though he would die someday, it wouldn't be from cancer. He began his usual stretching and exercise routine. When he felt like his body had had a good workout, he stopped and took a shower. Then he got into his wooden sauna to heat up the body temperature for his habitual length of time and jumped immediately afterward into a freezing cold shower, shocking his immune system into producing more white blood cells.

"Whew that felt good!" Dr. Benson said. Afterward, he drank a cup of echinacea tea to replenish lost fluids while he peacefully read the Bible to replenish his spirit and to honor God. This daily routine always made him feel virile. Now that he had discovered the cure for cancer, he knew he would have time to follow the routine every day. Hopefully, it would help him live even longer than Noah.

He suddenly had an urge to call his patient and friend John Hughes and tell him the good news about the cure.

"I knew you would be the one to find a cure for cancer!" Mr. Hughes said when the call went through. "Just like I knew I'd become a billionaire by making great business decisions."

"I knew it too! We need to meet as soon as possible. Please come to my house and meet me in my private laboratory," Dr. Benson said.

"But of course. I will take my helicopter!"

Before long, Mr. Hughes's helicopter landed on the Bensons' huge front lawn.

Adolfo ran out as soon as the helicopter's rotors stopped spinning. "Your bloody flying contraption ruined the lawn!" he cried.

Mr. Hughes's bodyguard tried to push Adolfo aside, thinking he might be a threat, but Adolfo was still nimble from all those years of ballet. He sidestepped the guard's lunge, untouched. The guard was judo-flipped by Joe who came to aid. The guard became angry and started to reach for his handgun, but Mr. Hughes grabbed the man's arm.

"No, stop!" he ordered. "We're sorry about the lawn, sir. I'm a cancer patient of Dr. Benson's. He's expecting me."

"Then why didn't you say so, sir? You could have prevented this oaf from exhibiting his violent tendencies!"

"We'll meet again!" the guard growled.

"I don't think so, because I'm not going to hell!" Adolfo shot back.

"All right, gentlemen, let's go on inside," said Mr. Hughes.

They all headed to the laboratory.

Dr. Benson conducted a CT scan and a CTC blood test on Mr. Hughes. The test results were good—no tumors, only cancer in the blood. He would not need to operate before beginning the new treatment. Dr. Benson administered the supercharged granulocytes by injection, followed by the rare plant enzyme. Then he instructed Mr. Hughes to consume some fresh echinacea from Olivia's garden. Dr. Benson also gave his patient a strict diet-and-exercise regimen and recommended the same hot sauna and cold shower routine he followed himself. He warned Mr. Hughes that he had to follow the instructions to the letter.

"This is one order I will gratefully follow, Dr. Benson. Thank you! And by the way, who was that English man?"

"That's my father-in-law, Adolfo. Why?"

"He certainly seems healthy and is quick on his feet for an old man."

"He is indeed. He once had cancer, but I cured him, thank God."

"It's you who found the cure for cancer, not God," Mr. Hughes corrected him. "You are the best doctor and scientist in the world. I'm going to send you a nice gift of thanks soon. Good-bye!"

The two friends shook hands, but the bodyguard kept his distance. Then Mr. Hughes and the guard departed on the helicopter.

17

D r. Benson continued to cure his patients. He spent several months preparing a presentation on his success to share with the world. He sealed all his medical secrets about diseases, viruses, and cancer in a floor safe in his mansion.

One day, when Dr. Benson had been seeing patients at the hospital, he noticed on his calendar that Mr. Hughes was his last appointment. His most recent CT scan and CTC blood test results were in.

"They're all negative," Dr. Benson was able to tell him when they met. "The tests show no cancer in your blood."

"Does this mean...I'm cured? No cancer? And I will live many more years as a rich and happy man?"

"Yes, sir! You are cured of cancer completely! You will live many more years. It's an honor to have been able to help you, and to help all of mankind be free of this horrible disease."

Mr. Hughes shook his hand, hugged him, and said, "Thank you, Doctor! Your cancer cure is going to be worth a fortune!"

Dr. Benson laughed. "I'm preparing to tell the world in a few weeks how to mass-produce the medication, and to explain the full regimen a person must follow to be cured. I will also explain how people can prevent ever acquiring cancer in the first place. It all begins with having a pure mind. A person must have a peace eternal, or the cancer could come back!"

"Stop talking in riddles! I know you live a comfortable life, Doctor, and that your wife also makes good money as a ballet dancer. But I'm talking about real money with this cure. An enormous amount of money! I will make you a billionaire. What do you say? Give me your research notes about the medication and regimen and let me be in charge of distribution. Imagine how powerful we could be!"

"No, Mr. Hughes, this cure is for everybody. To restrict it only to certain people would be to spit on my mother's grave!"

"I am a man of power, Doctor. I offer you a deal. If you do not give me what I demand, you will regret it. You have one of the greatest opportunities in history. All you need to do is submit to me, a man of considerable power and influence."

"Are you threatening me?"

Mr. Hughes touched his Water Mason ring subconsciously. "I'm simply telling you how it is, and what will become of you if you don't obey my request!"

"I have an important father, Mr. Hughes. You don't scare me. Get out!"

"You mean your father the general? Wowee!" Mr. Hughes laughed.

"No. I mean God, the Father Almighty. Good day to you, Mr. Hughes. Leave my office at once!"

Dr. Benson called security to escort Mr. Hughes from the hospital. Armed guards took him to his limousine. His personal bodyguards gave the hospital security the stink-eye. The hospital security showed no fear and gave the bodyguards the stink-eye right back. Some of them were tough, retired police officers who had seen it all.

Mr. Hughes got into his limousine and began to think. "If I can get my hands on that cancer cure, I will acquire power over many people and nations!" he murmured to himself. As his limo sped down the road, he let loose a thunderous, sadistic laugh—the laugh of a devil.

18

Handsome young Joe was at the mall with the Benson family. He was waiting on a bench with Rose for his mother to return from the bathroom when several beautiful young ladies approached him.

"What's your name?" they asked, fluttering around him.

"Joe," he answered simply, uninterested.

They commented on his nice hair and attractive eyes. One of them, a gorgeous blonde, said, "Would you like to walk around the mall with us?"

Rose stepped in. "Leave my brother alone! Mom! Mom!"

Olivia returned just then from the restroom. "Can I help you, ladies?"

"Your son is dreamy," they said, stroking his hair and giggling. "Can he walk around the mall with us?"

"He is too young for you. Bye!" said Olivia firmly. Then she grabbed Joe's hand and the three of them moved away.

Adolfo, who had been watching the scene from nearby, just laughed and walked toward them. They were all carrying many shopping bags. It had been a long day, and they were all tired.

Joe tapped his grandfather's shoulder. "Grandpa, those men are following us!"

Adolfo looked in the direction he pointed, but he only saw a few men who appeared to be purchasing things. "Those men are only shopping, Joe."

But Joe insisted. "No! I can feel what they are up to by using my spirit energy. They only want you to think they're buying something. They're tricking you!"

"I'm with you, Joe. Don't be afraid." He turned to Olivia. "Angel, I think the children are tired. How about finishing our trip some other day?"

"Joe, shall we go home for supper with your father and talk about the fine day we had?" she asked

"Yes, please. Let's go home!" Joe pleaded.

Olivia frowned. She seemed to feel that Joe was concerned about something.

They all went out to the parking lot, trying to remember where Olivia's Mercedes SUV was parked.

They found it and began loading their purchases in the trunk.

"Hurry, Mom. Let's go home!" Joe whined.

"Calm down. Be more like your sister, dear!"

Suddenly, three men tried to grab Joe and Rose. Athletic Adolfo was able to fight them off at first, with help from Joe, who used his aikido skills to trip one assailant into another. He put his samurai training to further use, by concentrating on where his opponent was going to move, and anticipating his motion. Joe had been developing this skill, which his sensei called body connection. His body connection was already so strong that he could move another person wherever he wanted. When two assailants came back at him from two different directions, Joe redirected one into the other, connecting two lines of energy and causing the two men to collide.

Joe, Rose, and Olivia got into the SUV safely, but before Adolfo could climb in one of the men pulled out a gun.

Adolfo lunged at him, crying, "Go, Olivia! Leave now!"

She obeyed her father's instructions, just as in the days when they had performed ballet together. She floored the gas pedal and screeched through the parking lot.

Joe fumbled with his and Rose's seatbelts, crying, "Go, Mom, go!"

Olivia heard gunshots behind them, but she didn't dare stop. She heard a police siren. She had a horrible sickening feeling in her stomach, but all she wanted to do at that moment was to get her children home safely.

Adolfo continued to fight the assailants using all the athletic skills he had, even though he felt fearfully hot and wet. He saw blood gushing from his stomach.

"Damn, the same place where I was cured of cancer is the same place this bloody bullet hit me! God, why?" he said aloud.

He dropped to his knees, mortally wounded. The three assailants started to kick him mercilessly. Through his pain, he heard a calming voice coming from the skies. He looked up and says, "Yes, Gabriel. I believe!"

The first Beverly Hills police officers on the scene found Adolfo clutching one of the assailants in a death grip. They leapt from their vehicle, handguns drawn, and formed an L-shaped cover position. The bad guys were positioned at the top. Two of the assailants were trying desperately to pry Adolfo off their buddy.

"Everybody put their hands up! Freeze!" a policeman shouted as the officers pointed their guns at the men.

One of the assailants shot at the rookie officer, hitting him in the face. The officer screamed in pain and fell to the ground.

His partner, who had been driving, shouted, "Jack, youngster, are you all right? Speak!"

There was no response. He called in on his radio, "Officer down! Shooting in progress, send backup with ambulance now!"

At last, the two assailants pried Adolfo's limp body away from their buddy. The three men began to move toward the lone officer. The officer fired, striking dead the assailant on the left to keep the other assailants to the right of him. One of the two jumped onto the roof of a nearby automobile and started shooting, striking the officer in the thigh and calf. The officer went into survival mode, taking a crouched position behind the engine of the police car and patiently waiting for the assailant on the roof to move. When he saw the assailant moving to another car roof, he aimed and shot, hitting him in the neck and chest. The assailant fell, lifeless, to the ground.

"Where the hell is my backup?" the officer asked, moving over to see how his partner Jack was doing while trying to get a read on the remaining assailant. He saw no sign of anyone.

Officer Bill found Jack lying in a pool of blood with his eyes open. He checked his partner's vitals—no pulse. He could hear sirens in the far distance. He saw mall security guards pointing at something behind him. The officer suddenly felt a hot, sharp pain in the back of his left shoulder. The final assailant had stabbed a sharp knife into the officer's flesh.

The officer attempted to shoot, but the assailant knocked his gun away. He tried to stab the officer in the chest next, but the officer used his natural reflexes and combat experience to grab the assailant's wrist. The officer's subconscious mind quickly flashed back to his time as an army ranger in Afghanistan. His military training and weight-lifting regimen paid off as he struggled. He succeeded in pinning the assailant to the ground. With his free hand, he pulled out his reserve .357-caliber snub-nose handgun from an ankle holster, and fired two shots into the assailant's belly. The assailant continued to struggle beneath with his deadly sharp knife, so the officer quickly buried the gun barrel deep into the man's neck and fired with the muzzle facing up toward the brain. The assailant's head exploded all over like a smashed watermelon.

Backup finally arrived, along with an ambulance.

"There are four dead men, along with one dead police officer. A total of five dead and one surviving, severely injured officer," an EMT reported to the police lieutenant.

The lieutenant walked up to the injured police officer who was lying on a gurney with medical staff assisting him. "You're going to have to account for all your rounds, per protocol."

The injured officer of grit and tolerance, muscular in built, but with the speed of a tiger, blinked to focus his eyes. Then, gathering his strength, he grabbed the lieutenant's shirt, pulled him in close, and said, "I have one bullet left. Do you want it?"

The lieutenant fearfully swallowed and squeezed the officer's hand.

"It's okay, Bill! Let's get you to a hospital, all right? You're a police officer. You're home. You're not in the war anymore." Bill, he knew, won a Silver Star in combat for heroism. Unfortunately, he has still suffered from post-traumatic stress disorder.

19

D r. Benson hastened home to console Olivia and the children when he learned that Adolfo had died of gunshot wounds. In the following week, the police conducted a thorough investigation but without finding out who the assailants might have been. A funeral was finally held, and Adolfo was buried next to his wife at the local Catholic cemetery rather than in his native England. Many of his colleagues from the ballet world came to honor him. At the graveside, the priest finished the service by saying, "God created man from the earth. Man came from it, and shall return to it. Amen."

Olivia cried as she held her husband; Napoleon and Lumbra held the children. Adolfo's casket was lowered slowly into the earth. The family members each dropped a handful of dirt on it. They departed for the memorial reception, which was to be held at the Benson mansion.

Olivia had delivered the eulogy for her father. More than anything, she said, the lesson that would stick with her was how he taught her to concentrate, to focus on a decision at hand, and to use that selective tunnel vision to accomplish her desires. This art of concentration had helped her much in life, she said, and her husband's ability to concentrate was also what had attracted her to him initially.

"My father will always be in my memories," she said. "His favorite saying was, 'A person who makes up his mind to use complete concentration with desire is omnipotent.'" She brushed away tears. "I am grateful that my husband has many of the same traits that my wonderful, caring father had. We must work to build memories every day, and live in the present while we are alive, so that we can take our memories with us into eternity. I believe that this way, when we are in heaven, we will have something to talk about."

The guests laughed gently.

"I thank you, everyone, for coming, and for honoring my loving father. Please enjoy the buffet of fruit, food, and beverages, and the photos of my father, the great dancer of the English Ballet Theatre!"

Many people paid their respects to Olivia and Dr. Benson and departed soon after she finished speaking, but others stayed to eat and reminisce about Adolfo.

Lumbra came in to tell Olivia that there was a phone call for her. It was General Benson, who offered his condolences and said he had only just heard the news a few hours ago. He had already booked a flight to California, though, and said he would be there as soon as he could.

There was one unwelcome guest at the wake—John Hughes. He was lurking in the shadows of the Bensons' yard with his bodyguards.

"You idiots!" he said to them. "You let one old man, a little boy, and only two police officers stop you from kidnapping Dr. Benson's kids! You're damn lucky I don't line up all you overpaid, so-called enforcers and shoot you dead myself! Now that you've had the opportunity to learn the layout of the Bensons' house, I'm ordering you to come back and retrieve what is rightfully mine. I want that cancer cure. I'm sure he has his notes hidden here somewhere!"

"Yes, I'm sure of it too," said the head guard. "But what if Dr. Benson tries to stop us?"

"Then you kill him and that beautiful wife he doesn't deserve!"

Suddenly, a warm bird dropping hit Hughes in the face and dripped into his mouth. Herbie was sitting on a tree branch just a few feet above him, listening.

Hughes picked up a small rock and threw it angrily at Herbie, but he missed.

"You bastard bird!"

———❦———

A month passed. The general, who had been staying with them since Adolfo's funeral, awoke early one morning. He thought of his beautiful jeep, with its reinforced armored plates around the body, sitting parked.

He said to himself, "Arnold feels like going for a drive!"

He asked if he could take Joe and Rose to Disneyland for the day.

At first, Dr. Benson felt uncertain about letting the children leave. Then he decided that, after the trauma of their grandfather's death, they probably needed a break. Besides, with the children out of the house, he could spend some quality time with Olivia. He told the general to go ahead, and then he went a step further and gave Napoleon and Lumbra the rest of the day and evening off. He, too, missed Adolfo, but he had good memories of him. Olivia's values were also a fine reflection of her father's parenting.

Dr. Benson hugged his children and said, "My strong son Joe and my pretty daughter Rose, never worry, you can feel the goodness of God's spirit and energy. It doesn't matter if you cannot see God. Knowing he is there is enough. Know too that Daddy's love and spirit energy will always be with you both. I love you, Joe! I love you, Rose! Now go have fun with your grandfather at Disneyland."

Joe and Rose hugged and kiss their father good-bye, and Dr. Benson sent them off with a big smile.

Dr. Benson couldn't wait to start the foreplay with Olivia. He wanted to hear her beautiful English voice whisper in his ear. Everyone had gone. He turned on the master bedroom's stereo system to his favorite Beatles song, "Let It Be," and set it to play on repeat. Olivia entered the bedroom in a negligee through which he could partially see her voluptuous, athletic body. At the bedside were two pitchers of fresh water from the garden well and a porcelain bowl filled with small squares of cut-up mangoes. There was only one fork to share. Dr. Benson lay on the bed as she came close. He couldn't decide whether to look at her beautiful face or gorgeous body, but then their eyes met and their spirits connected. He didn't remember how their clothes came off, but they soon found themselves making love vigorously, pausing only to drink water and eat mangoes for energy.

Later that afternoon, Dr. Benson arose and put on his robe, leaving Olivia to sleep. He felt very hungry.

There was no water or mango left, so he started walking downstairs to the kitchen. On his way, he thought about the international speech he would be giving in one week's time, describing how he discovered the cure for cancer. It would almost certainly mean another Nobel Prize and more fame and money, but he never set out to seek those. He wanted only to prevent other children from losing a parent to cancer the way he had. All the media would be there for the speech, which was good; that would help him acquire important contacts to help mass-produce the cancer cure for the millions. He felt secure, knowing that all his medical research was hidden in a safe in the garden. Only he and Olivia knew where it was, although he had seen that nosy Herbie flying around when he locked the materials in the safe. There was a safe in the house, naturally, but he knew that was the first place a thief would look so he had moved all his medical research out of it. Even if the worst happened and someone found it, all the medical information was safe in his head, of course.

Dr. Benson put his cell phone down on the kitchen counter.

"Yes! There are pomegranates!" he said out loud.

He poured himself some water and began to eat. When he had had his fill, he started back upstairs with a pomegranate in his robe pocket and two glasses of water. He suddenly realized that he had left his cell phone behind, but he shrugged and thought, *Oh, well, this way I won't be disturbed.*

He was about to wake Olivia to offer her some water when he heard a noise outside. *Is it the kids getting back from Disneyland this early?* he wondered. He knew that the general was a kid at heart and would probably try to stay at the park as long as time permitted.

Herbie started squawking on the balcony, so Dr. Benson went out to see what was bothering him. Down below, he saw four men in black ski masks kicking in the front door. He ran to the phone to dial 911, but the line was dead. He reached for his cell phone, but remembered that he had left it in the kitchen.

"Olivia!" he whispered, patting her shoulder. "Where's your cell phone?"

"I always leave it in my car," she said groggily. "Why?"

"We have intruders. Get dressed, darling. We may have to fight them."

She scrambled out of bed.

"Robert, I love you! Remember that everything happens for a reason. God is with us, my love!"

Dr. Benson felt grateful that his father had trained him for life-threatening emergencies. "You never know when you might find yourself on the battlefield," the general would always say. Dr. Benson grabbed a

Springfield M1911 pistol with an eight-round magazine full of special Black Talon ammunition and then told Olivia to hide in the closet.

"I have confidence in you!" she said, and then kissed him full on the mouth as if that kiss could be their last.

He stepped outside the room in a kneeling position, just like the general taught him. He could hear the men downstairs tearing up the place as if looking for something.

"God, please take care of our children, Joe and Rose," he prayed. "And please protect Olivia from these men!"

He crept forward to the steps until the men were in view. He pointed his gun at them but didn't want to hurt them if he didn't have to.

"Leave my house, please! I'm a doctor!" he shouted.

"There he is!" said one of the intruders.

They started coming upstairs. Herbie waddled into the bedroom to hide under the bed and eavesdrop as he always did.

"We want the cancer cure and all your research!" one intruder shouted.

Dr. Benson worriedly reached into his robe pocket and hurled the pomegranate at the closest man. The pomegranate hit him hard in his face and exploded in a mess of red juice and pulp.

"You son of a b——h!" the intruder said as he angrily wiped the pomegranate off his face with his shirtsleeve.

The evil intruders continued to move in the direction of the worried Dr. Benson.

"The police are on their way!" Dr. Benson shouted in what he hoped was a beguiling, confident voice.

"They'll be too late for you!" one of them said, pulling out his gun.

Thinking only of Olivia's safety, Dr. Benson began shooting at them while counting to three between each shot to calm himself like his father had taught him. He ignored their screams of pain. Three of the men fell. The last intruder, however, managed to get upstairs and disarm him.

"I should shoot you now for killing my three friends, but maybe if you hand over the cure I'll spare your life," he threatened.

Dr. Benson wanted the killing to stop, so he said, "All the materials are in a safe. If I give them to you, do you promise that I will not be harmed? And that you will leave immediately?"

The man's lips glistened with saliva. "You have my word."

Dr. Benson took the man to the bedroom safe and gave him papers that, to an untrained eye, would resemble the cancer cure information.

The intruder grabbed the papers and said, "Dr. Benson, I regret that I must do this, but John Hughes said I must kill you. He wanted me to tell you that power is all that matters, and now that this power is his, you don't matter anymore."

He coldly fired his gun at Dr. Benson.

Blood pours out from wounds in Dr. Benson's chest and head. He felt wet and warm all over, and he tasted blood on his lips as he looked at the ceiling. Olivia screamed and came out of the closet to hold him. The assailant fired more gunshots and Olivia fell on her husband, lifeless. In his peripheral vision, Dr. Benson saw Herbie flap out the window. The intruder fired at the bird, but Herbie escaped. The man departed.

Dr. Benson was crying and in enormous pain. Suddenly, he saw a light above him and felt warm. He looked up and saw the angel Gabriel smiling down upon him. With all the strength remaining in his good, honest heart, Dr. Benson held Olivia close and whispered, "Yes, Gabriel, I have always believed."

Dr. Benson's eyes flickered as he faded away into eternal peace.

20

General Benson's armored jeep came up the driveway. His military experience immediately told him that something was wrong. He grabbed his Desert Eagle .50-caliber from underneath his car seat and told Joe and Rose to get down on the floor. Joe helped Rose crouch down below the seats. General Benson suddenly saw a man in a black ski mask running out of the house, holding a gun and some paperwork. The general slipped out of the jeep and squatted behind it for protection.

"Stop!" the general called. "Put your hands in the air!"

The henchman started running and began to fire lead bullets in the general's direction. Sparks flew into the air as the assailant's bullets hit the armored jeep. Then General Benson shot back, and the man's head and chest exploded into the air like a pumpkin full of firecrackers.

The police arrived and discovered the four dead intruders, the open safe, and the bodies of Dr. and Mrs. Benson. They quickly ruled the incident an attempted burglary resulting in homicide, and acknowledged that General Benson had shot in self-defense. They began their investigation, but to General Benson and his grandchildren, the only important fact in the case was already known—their loved ones were dead!

—⁓—

The funeral of Robert and Olivia Benson was a tragic one. Joe and Rose grieved loudly. They were surrounded by many entertainers, celebrities, politicians, physicians, and biologists. The mayor of Beverly Hills and the Beverly Hills police chief both attended to offer their condolences. The family attorney, Basil Hermes, was charged with giving the eulogy.

"Dr. Robert Benson and his beautiful wife, the ballet star Olivia Benson, lived great lives and made the most of their time here on earth. Now they are blessed to be in heaven with God our creator. Amen!"

General Arnold Benson, unable to control his military bearing, slumped over the top of his son's casket, weeping copiously. "Robert, my son, I will miss you! I promise you I will avenge your murder!"

There was no reception, so the mourners proceeded directly to the cemetery. The two caskets were lowered ceremoniously into the ground. The Bensons were buried next to Dr. Benson's mother, Mary. Piles of beautiful flowers were placed upon the graves, in honor of Olivia's love of flowers and plants.

—⚬—

Time passes to heal the grieving Benson family. Since General Benson had become responsible for raising his grandchildren, he had announced his retirement. He had many good values, and people enjoyed listening to him speak and asking him questions. General Benson had a right frame of mind, a peace eternal. His comrades and fellow officers hosted a party to celebrate the five-star general's career. General Benson received a commemorative gold plaque by a surprise guest— the commander-in-chief himself, the president of the United States. The plaque pictured a general saluting with a sword. The president read the engraving on the plaque aloud.

"The United States of America is honored to acknowledge the service of Five-Star General Arnold Benson. General Benson exemplified honor for country, from the valor he showed at West Point to his last assignment working directly for the president at the White House."

The guests clapped. The president saluted General Benson and handed him the plaque. The other officers in attendance lined up to shake General Benson's hand and offer him their congratulations on his fine career. A buffet of fine cuisine awaited them with the White House's own vintage beer.

—∞—

One day, not long after General Benson's retirement had begun, he sat in his late daughter-in-law's beautiful garden, smoking a Honduran cigar. Suddenly, Herbie landed on a nearby tree and began to talk.

"Hand over the cure! Awk! John Hughes said I must kill you!"

Tears came rushing from General Benson's eyes like miniature waterfalls. He took a few breaths to calm himself. Now he knew who had Robert and Olivia murdered. He wasted no time. He hired three former Green Berets to keep watch over Joe and Rose, and began to make plans for revenge. He also retained Napoleon and Lumbra to maintain a sense of normalcy at the house. They would keep the children fed and the home clean.

General Benson hired a private jet from a retired air force general friend and flew to Mason, Ohio. A friend, General Tom, was the pilot.

"It's been a while since we've seen each other, Arnold," General Tom said. "How do you like it up here in these big blue skies with clouds you could touch like smoke?"

"I sure do like it. And I appreciate your taking me to Ohio on such short notice."

They drank coffee and enjoyed the scenery together.

When the jet landed, General Tom said, "I'm going to see some family here in Mason. Just call me on my cell phone when you're ready to go back to Los Angeles."

"Thank you, Tom." General Benson's cell phone, Red Baby, glowed bright red as it listened to the conversation from the generals closed dark front shirt pocket.

General Benson picked up a small cloth-covered box and made his way to the temple of the Water Masons, which was in the heart of the beautiful city. It was where all high-ranking Masons gathered for important meetings. General Benson, a Water Mason leader himself, had requested an emergency meeting with the group's other leaders. General Benson walked up the steps to the huge front double doors of the Water Mason temple, and he saw two large men in white suits wearing cowls with pig-like facial features. This must be a new security measure, to conceal their true identity, for they looked as if they came out of some laboratory.

The general says, "I guess it's Halloween?" The two men say nothing, so he flashes his Water Mason sign with his hand. The two men observe his Water Mason ring as they make a light-hearted animal squeal—the sound of a pig. They bow their large covered cowl heads to General Benson, and the huge double doors just open up mysteriously. The general makes his way down the corridor and hears a sound of someone gasping for air. As visually the general sees the stage in the hall's Waterfall Room was being set up by diligent Chinese American workers dressed in historic railroad uniforms. The general entered in a formal military class-A uniform. Suddenly, he witnessed a horror. He observed a bloody beaten man being dragged away by two abnormally huge muscular men wearing black tunics. The general noticed the beaten man's head bobbled with lifelessness, as one of his blue eyes dangled from its socket while puffed up like a bloody marshmallow. The general instantly smells disinfectant in the air, as he continues walking in defensive mode. He spots three maids of three different ethnicities—Mexican American, African-American, and Irish American—dressed in the Colonial era clothing, cleaning up blood-borne pathogens. The three maids diligently finish cleaning, then one by one walk up to the Water Mason's grand commander. The grand commander smiles at them as each maid kisses him on the lips then walk away clacking on their wooden Dutch shoes.

He continued to walk as he approached the Water Mason altar. It contained an artificial waterfall. Below it was a small pond where there was sculpture of John the Baptist baptizing Jesus Christ. Adjacent to the altar, the assembled leaders waited for him to speak in this huge hall. They sat in an authentic relic meeting table of late King George.

General Benson took a breath then he placed the covered box on the altar. He stood in the huge meeting hall with his commanding presence and gazed at everyone. Then he repeated the two mottos of the Water Masons.

"Number one. Water must flow with honor. We must live with honor, just like flowing water will never goes stale, people must live with honor. Number two. Follow the Golden Rule. Do unto others as you would have them do unto you."

He addressed the full group of Water Masons but seemed to direct his voice especially toward the grand commander who sat by himself on a throne at the head of the hall. Light from a skylight shaped like the holy cross fell upon the general as he spoke.

"What we do for ourselves alone dies with us. What we do for others and the world, though, remains and is immortal! I requested that John Hughes be excluded from this private meeting. I tell you today that John Hughes had my only son, Dr. Robert Benson, murdered for his own selfish reasons. Hughes wanted to steal the cancer cure my son had been working on his whole life. My brothers, I want you to know that my Robert never lost sight of his chief aim in this life, which was to cure fatal diseases."

He pointed to the covered box on the altar.

"I offer you exhibit A as evidence of John Hughes's guilt."

He removed the cloth cover to reveal a birdcage. Herbie the parrot was in it, nibbling on some seeds.

"Herbie," the general asked, "what happened to Dr. Benson?"

Herbie just whistled. The Water Masons began to look askance at General Benson, as if to see whether he was mad or whether this was some kind of joke.

"Herbie, what did you hear about Dr. Benson?" he asked again.

"Hand over the cure!" Herbie said, loud and clear. "John Hughes said I must kill you!"

The room became very quiet.

The grand commander said, "Arnold, what is it you ask of us?"

With tears streaming down his face, the general said, "I respectfully request to have Water Mason member John Hughes eliminated. First, he never had authorization from the Water Masons to target and kill my son. Robert may not have been a Water Mason, but I am! Second, Robert was a biologist and physician who worked all his life to bring light into the world. He would often say, 'Eliminate all unnecessary desires to achieve your ultimate goal in life!' He repeated this to himself often so the message would penetrate his subconscious and help him achieve positive results. Is that not a noble goal? Should not his murder be avenged?" General Benson paused to gather his strength. "Water must flow with honor! Help me! Helfen Sie mir!" The general, now sobering hard, reflects back on his wife and boy, Robert.

One by one, all the Water Masons stood up. The grand commander was the last to stand. With one voice, they cried, "Eliminate!"

General Benson now knew what he had to do as Red Baby glowed bright red. He called Tom from the temple and asked when they could leave.

"I'll meet you at the airport in thirty minutes," Tom said. "I've been expecting your call."

—⁓—

On the jet, the general broke down a little. "I still miss my son," he confessed.

Tom responded with a leader's comforting, soothing voice. "Just sit back and relax. I have some one hundred percent agave tequila, and some pillows and blankets. God has a reason for everything!"

General Benson tossed back a shot of tequila and sucked on a salted lemon while he comforted himself among the clean blankets and pillows. He gazed out at the clouds and blue skies and said, "Step on it, Tom, I want to see my grandchildren!"

The jet hummed with enormous speed as it flew through clouds and over mountains. They finally arrived at the Los Angeles airport.

The general shook his old friend's hand and said, "Thank you, Tom, keep in touch."

"Anytime, Arnold. Call me when you want to play a few rounds of golf and talk."

General Benson gathered up Herbie's cage in his arms and stepped into his armored jeep. He headed back toward Beverly Hills.

Herbie made a ruckus, constantly saying, "Let me out, let me out!" With one hand on the wheel, the general opened the cage. "Thanks, General! You're a real general!"

"You're welcome, Herbie. Relax and enjoy the ride."

General Benson thought about all the guidelines set forth by Robert and Olivia in the living trust. He would endeavor to fulfill them all. He would also initiate a mission of revenge to eliminate Water Mason member John Hughes. He knew he must act quickly, before his window of opportunity closed.

Arriving home, the general exited his armored jeep while carrying Herbie and his luggage. He communicated with his three Green Berets using a glowing Red Baby palm phone that was tucked in a buttoned pocket on his shirt front.

"Activate voice seven six three!" General Benson commanded the phone. The Berets were in position— one on the roof, two inside the mansion. They informed him that Joe and Rose were fine, and the coast was all clear. The general found Rose playing piano and Joe practicing with his sword, swiping fiercely at an imaginary foe. The two children had become closer to each other since their parents' passing. The general greeted them with hugs and kisses.

"Grandfather, Grandfather, we missed you! Please don't leave us again!" they said with tears in their eyes.

"Grandfather is home for good. I will never leave you."

At that moment, Herbie flew around them and said, "Grandfather's home!"

He landed on Rose's piano, and the children caressed and kissed him.

Lumbra came in and took the general's luggage. She smiled and walked away.

Napoleon entered and said, "Filet mignon for dinner, Sir General." As usual, he finished his sentence with a loud pop, striking his puckered mouth with his hand.

The general sat down for dinner with Joe and Rose and listened to all their stories. Following this quality time together, Lumbra escorted the children off to bed. Napoleon took a coffee pot to the study, and the general retired there for the rest of the evening.

He pulled a cigar from his pocket and smelled it. "Mm-mmm. Honduran."

He began puffing on the delicious cigar and sipping a cup of joe. He brainstormed ways to eliminate John Hughes with all the powers of his imagination. He was in a deep thought process moment. At last he said aloud, "Aha! I know how to do it!"

21

General Benson gathered his Green Berets for a mission-planning meeting behind closed doors in the study. He gave the soldiers equipments: full-body armor, cell phone-jamming devices, gas masks, eagle-vision binoculars, rope, chemical-agent grenades, olive-green FNP-45 tactical handguns with Trijicon RMR sights, handgun magazines that could hold fifteen rounds of .45-caliber Black Talon bullets, and sharp large Bowie knives.

"You will use only God-given methods for communicating with each other on this mission, such as hand signals or speech. No phones or radios can be used due to the radio- and cell phone-jamming devices that will be in place. You will notice that there are no silencers on the handguns. I want John Hughes to hear you coming for him. I want him to feel fear all the way up until the moment when he is eliminated. Understood?"

"Yes, sir, General, sir!" They responded in unison.

General Benson used his high-tech palm cell phone Red Baby to hack into John Hughes's computer. He reviewed all of the documents and e-mails on his hard drive.

"Yes! Red Baby, you are much better than the old iPad or iPhone systems!" General Benson said. He was very pleased with the intelligence of the engineers at the Saman Corporation who had invented the phone. The glowing beautiful solar-powered Red Baby kept tabs on General Benson's high blood pressure, and he had it set to give him voice-activated reminders of appointments on his calendar. General Benson used it religiously.

Among the information he found when hacking into John Hughes's computer was background data on his security personnel. General Benson saw only one man who was likely to give them problems—a highly trained ex-marine with experience in the Gulf War.

"He won't panic," the general cautioned his men. "He might even inspire his own men to fight hard against you." He went on to reassure them that the man would only be a temporary nuisance. He told them he believed they would succeed in this mission because they were Green Berets.

The men gave a shout that sounded like a grizzly growling. "Huurrrr!"

The general handed out thermometers, wax, and lighters. The men broke the thermometers and poured the mercury onto the tips of the Black Talon bullets that were laid out on a desk. The men were careful not to knock over any bullet or spill the mercury. With their cigarette lighters, they melted wax over the tips of the bullets to keep the liquid mercury from coming off until the bullets struck a target. When the mercury was released, it would poison the victim.

"This mission has a name," the general said. "Operation Eliminate John Hughes!" He handed a note to each of the three Berets. "The first man to come in contact with John Hughes is to read him this note prior to his elimination!"

The Berets, perfect soldiers of war, put on their body armor and loaded their guns with the mercury-tipped bullets. The general exchanged his jeep's real license plate for an old plate he had found at a junkyard in the city of Watts. He put a piece of brown paper over the plates, knowing it would fly off while he drove down the road.

The general had timed the mission perfectly for when Joe and Rose would still be at school, Lumbra in classes at her college, and Napoleon out buying groceries. No one was there to witness their preparations except Herbie, who sat on Rose's piano and watched them leave the study. Silence fell over the conservatory as they stood, ready to deploy. A fountain trickled quietly in the background and soft lighting illuminated the piano.

Herbie suddenly began to hop on the piano keys, as if playing a tune. He sang, "Be safe, Grandpa General! Avenge the doctor! Please come back!" He stopped and looked at them.

They all started laughing.

"Herbie," the general said, "you sing your parrot heart out! Don't worry, I'll be back."

They exited the mansion through a back door and got into the general's jeep. The three Green Berets slunk down low in the jeep, so nobody could see them as they drove down the road. General Benson turned the security cameras that monitored the large manor house back on by remote from his Red Baby cell phone.

They drove toward John Hughes's estate. The brown paper covering the old license plates fell off after several blocks. The general maintained a safe speed as they approached, so they wouldn't draw any attention to themselves. He parked the jeep a half block away, and let the Berets out by some trees and bushes, when there were no other cars or people around. It was the afternoon, so most people were away at work. General Benson departed last and alone, leaving his men to start mission: Operation Eliminate John Hughes.

As he drove away, he put on a CD of an orchestra playing "The Ballad of the Green Berets." The general sang along, visualizing his soldiers' success in eliminating the bastard John Hughes for killing his innocent son and daughter-in-law.

—✽—

The three Green Berets approached John Hughes's mansion. It was helpful that the property was on the outskirts of Beverly Hills; it meant very few people were likely to be around. The team put the jamming devices in place and set them to block all cell phone and radio signals within a half-mile radius. The team also cut the phone lines and internet cables to the house. With grappling hooks, they scaled the property's perimeter wall. Their body armor camouflaged them perfectly. They looked through their binoculars and spotted a helicopter on a landing pad, several uniformed security guards walking around with dogs, and various security cameras monitoring the area. The Berets were actually glad about the security cameras—part of their mission was to allow John Hughes to see and hear them coming to eliminate him.

Beret One was the team leader; he had the most combat experience. He checked himself and his men to see that all their body armor and gas masks were on properly and concealed their identities. They all gave each other a thumbs-up.

They noticed several security guards coming out of the Hughes's mansion, pointing to their inoperative cell phones and walkie-talkies. The Berets smiled. They arranged themselves into a three-point formation and charged, each holding a Bowie knife in one hand and a FNP-45 tactical handgun in the other. The Trijicon RMR sights mounted on their handguns allowed them to run and shoot with both eyes open. They started shooting. When they met a security guard or a dog, they hacked away at their heads, necks, arms, and legs with the knives to immobilize or kill them. They continued to shout "Hhhurrr!"

Beret Two smashed the inside of the helicopter's flight-control system to ensure it would stay grounded. Some of the security guards managed to shoot at them, but the body armor repelled their bullets.

As they entered the huge mansion, slashing at more guards and dogs, they found the ex-marine lying in wait. He fired a .50-caliber Desert Eagle at them. A bullet ripped through Beret Three's armor, killing him. Berets One and Two dropped to the ground and began to crawl as the marine continued shooting at them. He ran out of bullets after a few minutes, and the Berets fled the room. The marine opened a desk drawer, looking for more .50-caliber ammunition.

"Charge!" Beret One ordered. He and Beret Two rushed back in, attacking the marine and forcing him to drop his Desert Eagle to the ground. The marine was a good fighter, however, and managed to judo-flip Beret Two in the direction of Beret One, who dodged just in time.

"Nice try, marine!" he shouted.

War hero Beret One sliced deep into the marine's thigh with the Bowie knife, cutting deep into his nerves.

"Uh Rrr!" cried the marine, in pain.

Beret Two attempted to shoot the fighting marine but was somehow disarmed. Beret One tried to shoot him in the head, but he ducked and moved toward him. Beret One fired off another quick shot, and a mercury-laced Black Talon bullet entered the marine's uninjured leg.

"Ahhh!" he cried.

Before Beret One could fire another bullet, the marine disarmed him. Beret Two grabbed the marine from behind in a full nelson as Beret One thrust his sharp Bowie knife up into the marine's heart. The marine's eyes opened wide and then blinked, as if saying good-bye. Beret One felt the marine's last breath of air hit him in the face as he crumpled to the floor. The Green Berets both felt a brief pang of guilt—the marine was an admirable fighter, and he had believed he was fighting a just cause. He had died with honor.

The Green Berets retrieved their knives and guns from the floor. Beret One cut down a marine flag hanging in the foyer and laid it over the dead soldier.

They heard movement in the next room. With weapons at the ready, they moved carefully toward the noise. There they found John Hughes cowering pitifully and holding an open briefcase full of money.

"This is a million dollars in cash, and I have signed two five-million dollar bonds. Each of you could cash them at the Beverly Hills Bank. I signed them, look! That's five million dollars for each of you. Please, just don't hurt me!"

The Berets looked at each other and laughed.

"We're Green Berets! We don't care about money!" said Beret Two. "We do this for the thrill and excitement of highly dangerous missions. So you see, rich old man, we can't be bribed. Our boss knows we can never be deterred from our mission, unfortunately for you!"

Green Beret One pulled General Benson's note from his pocket and began to read it. "Mr. John Hughes, I regret that I must do this, but General Arnold Benson ordered me, with the Water Masons' blessing, to eliminate you!"

John Hughes had tears in his eyes as he said, "Water must flow with honor. I should have followed the Golden Rule!"

He started to hyperventilate in panic, and his eyes were blinking extremely quickly. The Green Berets began to shoot without further warning. The mercury-tipped .45-caliber Black Talon bullets hit Hughes in the abdomen, chest, and head. He fell down hard, in a pool of his own blood.

The Green Berets took deep breaths to calm themselves. They retrieved their fallen comrade's body so as not to leave any evidence that could link them— or General Benson—to the murder. They stole one of John Hughes's vehicles and drove away from the scene of battle.

—⚏—

General Benson parked his jeep in a secluded place by the ocean, took the old license plates off, and threw them into the water. He put the original license plates back on. He lit a cigar and puffed on it while looking at the waves.

—⚏—

Later that day, Joe and Rose were working on their homework while General Benson sat in the study sipping a cup of joe. A news report flashed on the television about the slaying of billionaire John Hughes. Police detectives were baffled as to why Hughes had been found dead in his study holding nothing but a briefcase filled with a million dollars in cash. It had clearly not been a robbery.

Beverly Hills Police Chief Donald Weber had been the first officer to arrive on the scene. He lived alone in a small ranch-style brick home on the outskirts of the city. He had plans to retire at the end of the year. He reported that all security film footage of the homicide had been destroyed by a computer virus. Chief Weber also happened to be a computer specialist and an active member of the Water Masons. There was no evidence leading to who had done this to Hughes or what the motive could have been—all that was known was that he had been eliminated.

Moments before the report aired, General Benson had received a text message on his phone.

> Operation Eliminate accomplished with one casualty—Beret Three.

The general glanced at the TV and smiled to himself. He sent a voice text back using his Red Baby phone.

> Congratulations! You men have given the Benson family honor. Thank you. You will find a generous donation in both of your bank accounts. The family of Beret Three will find a substantial sum in his account as well. From this moment on, there will be no more contact between us. Auf wiedersehen, my Green Berets!

A few moments later, General Benson's phone glowed red to indicate that he had an incoming call. It was from Donald Weber. The general answered without speaking, for security reasons.

"Water must flow with honor!" Chief Weber said.

"Continue, brother."

"Every-thing's been taken care of. Evidence eliminated!"

General Benson removed a Honduran cigar from his shirt pocket, smelled it, and said, "Beautiful, my brother. Those two five-million dollar bonds from John Hughes should only be cashed at our Water Mason brother's bank, the Beverly Hills Bank."

"Thank you, Arnold, but I took the million dollars in cash. That should tide me over for a while. I can't wait till I retire later this year! That money sure will pad my pension!"

General Benson puffed on his cigar. "There must be no more contact between us, Donald. I'm sorry, but that's an order. Auf wiedersehen, Chief Weber!"

22

On Monday, at around 4:00 p.m., General Benson left Joe and Rose with Napoleon, who was going to give them an early dinner. He had a mandatory Water Mason meeting at the Beverly Hills Bank. Before departing, he instructed the chef to call him should any emergency arise.

"Oui, monsieur," said Napoleon, again making his trademark popping noise. *Pop!* He served the children a dinner of fresh fruit, steamed vegetables, and cheese crepes.

"Humph," said Napoleon when he saw Joe trying to hide his Japanese sword under the table. "You know your grandfather's rule."

"Yes, but please! My instinct told me to bring it to the meal today!"

"Very well, just this once. You and Rose must practice proper manners while you eat at this table, just as if you lived in France, my country!"

He looked at his watch and smiled, for he knew that the love of his life, Lumbra, would be home soon from class.

Before long, he heard her pull up the drive in Olivia's old Mercedes SUV. The general gave it to her after Olivia's death, so that she could be self-sufficient, and make archaeological expeditions to places a normal car couldn't go.

Lumbra did not notice the black Honda Accord with no license plates parked at the bottom of the driveway. A white male of about thirty years old got out of the car after she passed, and stealthily approached the front door.

Lumbra was halfway inside the foyer when she remembered she'd left a book in the car that she wanted to show her Napoleon. Though she was eager to eat his delicious dinner, she returned to the front door. There was the stalker, staring at her. She gasped.

"Who are you and what do you want?"

"I want you!" he cried, flicking open a switchblade with his right hand. Lumbra tried to close the door, but the strong man blocked it with his foot.

Lumbra screamed and ran to the kitchen. "Help! Help!" she cried.

When Joe saw the man with the knife, he grabbed his sword. He swung it at him, cutting the man's arm.

"You little scum!" the man yelled as his blood dripped on the floor.

Napoleon pushed Lumbra and Rose out of the kitchen. "Call the police!" he yelled.

Joe adopted a samurai stance. The stalker dropped his switchblade and grabbed a meat cleaver from the counter. He swung it at Joe, but Joe easily moved out of the way thanks to the athletic ability he inherited from his mother.

Napoleon grabbed the sword away from young Joe and said, "Go protect the women, Joe, please!" Joe obeyed, running out of the kitchen to find Rose and Lumbra.

Napoleon wanted to give himself more room to fight, so he backed out the kitchen's rear door while keeping the sword in position, ready to strike. The stalker followed him into the conservatory.

"Get out now!" Napoleon shouted. "The police are coming!"

The evil man sauntered as he violently shouted terrible explicit vulgarism. Then he finally said, "I'm sick with cancer—so I'll do what I want. I want that pretty lady. Giver her to me and I'll leave!"

Napoleon knew he must use the skills that won him the Olympic silver medal in fencing years ago. Behind him was a staircase that led to the upstairs bedrooms. At the top of the stairs was a balcony overlooking the foyer. Joe, Rose, Herbie, and Lumbra were gathered there, watching Napoleon defend the Benson household. Lumbra pushed the preset 911 button on her cell phone, talked quickly, and was assured that the police were on the way. It was a good thing General Benson had prepared her and the rest of the family for emergencies.

Without warning, the stalker lunged at Napoleon with the cleaver for a death kill. Fortunately, Napoleon saw the evil man telegraphing his moves. He used a powerful parry-quinte—a complex defense against a fast-moving attack. Napoleon had enough. He feinted his sword at the stalkers head. It instantly drew a response from the assailant to defend his head, which left his lower torso open for any attack. Napoleon gained a beat in distance as he changed his swords direction in midflight from high to low, thrusting his sword deeply into the man's floating ribs or upper abdomen. The stalker shouted in pain and fell hard on the floor, in a pool of his own blood.

At that moment everyone heard the police sirens.

"You're the man, Napoleon!" Joe shouts.

"Awk! You're the man!" Herbie agreed.

Rose clung to Joe for comfort, while Lumbra ran down to Napoleon.

"Mi amor, te amo!" she cried, hugging and kissing him.

The police entered the house with guns drawn. Napoleon dropped the sword.

"Self-defense, officer," he said. "There's your criminal. Please get that evil man out of here!"

The officers cuffed Napoleon and put the injured stalker on a stretcher. Together they all left the mansion.

—⚋⚋—

The Beverly Hills police detained Napoleon for questioning but removed his handcuffs during the interview and soon released him. The stalker was identified as Jeb Wood, a parolee wanted for various crimes. He was arrested at the hospital, where he was being treated for wounds sustained in the confrontation. The physicians, upon learning that he had terminal cancer, also begin to treat the evil-spirited Jeb Wood for that—at the taxpayers' expense.

"I don't care about anybody, not even my parents. I don't care if I go to hell!" Jeb said.

At that moment, the police officers looked at the physicians, realizing it was going to be a long night.

"Hey, doc, do you have a cup of joe?" one officer asked.

—✦—

General Benson was alarmed to see police cars at the house when he returned from his meeting. They explained what had happened as he hugged and kissed his grandchildren.

"We looked at the surveillance video for evidence," one of the officers said.

The general watched the tape and saw Napoleon defending himself and the family. He also saw that Napoleon had tried to avoid the conflict by telling the attacker to leave, although he of course refused. The intruder clearly had intent to harm Napoleon and abduct Lumbra.

Detective McHorn took complete statements from Napoleon, Lumbra, Joe, and Rose in the presence of General Benson, who had been a judge advocate general in his younger days. After getting everyone's statements and reviewing the surveillance video again, the police departed the Benson residence, satisfied that they gotten their man.

Everyone was quiet after the police left, except Joe who had to vocalize his admiration of Napoleon's fencing skills.

"I thought you were only a chef!" he said.

Herbie, eavesdropping as always, said, "Only a chef! Only a chef!"

"That bird is a piece of work," Napoleon said.

Joe smiled. "Napoleon, please teach me what you know about sword fighting!"

"My sport is called fencing. It would be an honor to teach you, if your grandfather will allow me."

Joe looked at his grandfather pleadingly; the general melted a little. "Of course you have my permission, Joe. Maybe he'll teach you how to cook too!"

"I think only fencing," Napoleon said. "With all due respect, Joe, please stay out of my kitchen!"

The general had a good, hard laugh. Then he opened up to Joe.

"The more you learn about anything, Joe, the more you will be able to overcome adversities in this evil world. A pure, healthy mind comes from peace, happiness, and thinking only good thoughts. You will not escape harming your spirit if you do good deeds but think evil thoughts. Evil thoughts tempt you into evil actions, and that's what the devil wants, Joe. Practice thinking good thoughts, not bad, evil thoughts. Or you could get sick with diseases like cancer," General Benson said.

Joe looked at his grandfather and smiled in admiration. The general couldn't help noticing that Joe bore a remarkable resemblance to his father, Robert. He smiled back at his grandson, immensely pleased.

23

The fencing lessons began on Joe's thirteenth birthday. This year, it fell on a Sunday morning. He and Napoleon would begin training right after breakfast. Lumbra brought Joe a special breakfast in bed that Napoleon had created just for his birthday.

"Wow!" Joe said when he saw the food.

Lumbra kissed Joe on his cheek. "Happy birthday, Joe!"

Joe quickly consumed the French crepes Napoleon had filled with cream cheese, walnuts, fruits, and vegetables. Then he drank his tall glass of mineral water, burped, and began to pray.

"Dear Lord, thank you for this delicious food and drink. I wish my mother and father were here for my birthday! Lord, please take care of Mommy and Daddy. I love you, God! Amen."

Relaxed and at peace, Joe got dressed and then went downstairs to meet his grandfather.

General Benson hugged Joe with tears in his eyes. "Happy birthday, Joe! I gave you a constructive gift. It's waiting for you in the gym. Napoleon and Rose will see you there."

"Thank you for being here, Grandfather!" Joe said.

Joe was a teenager in complete awe of Napoleon's swordsmanship. He found new fencing gear waiting for him in the gym—a protective vest, sleek clothing that allowed mobility, a face mask, gloves, and shoes. He already had a variety of sabers, foils, and épées that his grandfather had purchased for him. The generous general had also bought Napoleon new equipment, too, since his own equipment, along with his Olympic silver medal, was back home with his father in France.

A piano in the gym had also been polished and tuned for Rose.

Rose came into the gym holding a small bowl of mixed nuts. She carried Herbie on her shoulder.

"Since its Joe's birthday, can I play some music for Joe and watch? Please, Napoleon? Please, Joe?" she asked.

"I always listen to music when I'm in the kitchen creating my masterpieces, so why not while I'm fencing?" Napoleon agreed. "Happy birthday, Joe!" Pop went his mouth.

"It is my birthday, and I like your piano-playing," Joe seconded. "It always makes me feel good when I hear you play music, my sister."

Joe scooped a few nuts from Rose's bowl and squeezed her shoulder. Joe and Rose had grown closer since their parents were killed. Rose sat down at the piano with Herbie. They flipped through Rose's favorite sheet music—works by Beethoven, Bach, Mozart, and Joaquín Rodrigo.

"I will play Father's favorite!" Rose said.

A few tears trickled down her lovely face. She still missed her father and mother deeply. Rose had a serious personality and an inner spirit like her mother, Olivia. She could sense what people were thinking before they spoke, also like her mother. She enjoyed making people feel good through music. Rose had even already developed an inspiring playing style that set her apart from any other musician.

"Listen and follow your heart!" Rose said cheerfully as she began to play the exquisite, uplifting music of Joaquín Rodrigo.

"Listen carefully, Joe," Napoleon said. "Fencing originally came from France."

"Can I learn to fence with the saber, please?"

"You will learn to use all three fencing swords well!" Napoleon promised. He showed Joe how to hold a fencing sword properly. "Hold it as if holding a small bird. Not too tight. Now, en garde, Joe!"

"What does en garde mean?"

"It means 'on your guard.'"

"You're a master swordsman, Napoleon! You must have a lot of awards."

"Well, the highest award I ever received was the Olympic silver medal, but I'm more proud of my numerous cooking awards."

"But Napoleon, anybody can eat! Not everybody can use a sword like I saw you do against that bad man. Why didn't you win the gold medal?"

"Well, remembering back in time. I believe now that it was because I telegraphed my moves. The German fencer who was my opponent said something to me that got me mad."

Joe remembered something Sensei Musashi had taught him: *Joe, use the way! Follow the Zen path! A person must know himself to have peace and harmony in whatever he does. Allowing someone else to control your emotions is not the way!*

Napoleon and Joe both put chest protectors on, then slipped into their white fencing uniforms and helmets. They each wore a glove on their right hand. Napoleon began by teaching Joe how to salute with a sword then how to shake hands after a bout like gentlemen. They got into the en garde position.

Rose looked up and down the piano keyboard. She looked at her friends—keys A through G. Rose located middle C and shouted, "On guard! Ready! Fence!" She started playing a light melody on her piano, while Herbie moved left and right along the top of it, making bird sounds. The reading of music sheets, the feel of the piano keys, and the sound of music reaching her ears give Rose the feeling of peace eternal.

"Joe, the blade should be in line with your arm. The pommel, or handle, goes through the valley of the palm to the wrist. The thumb lies on the top of the pommel. The index finger knuckle should be one finger-width from the bell guard," Napoleon said. "This, along with good footwork, keeps distance between you and your opponent, so he can't strike or harm you. Speed, accuracy, and timing take time to learn, but you will learn them. We will practice every chance we get. Good thing you have an open mind for learning, just like a Frenchman!"

Napoleon and Joe began to duel, moving in harmony to the beautiful Joaquín Rodrigo music that Rose was playing. As they fenced, Joe blended his samurai techniques with the new fencing techniques he was learning.

Napoleon eventually defeated Joe and said, "I bested you with a doublé. Here, let me show you."

He demonstrated the move, a counter parry that used a full-circular movement on the attacker's blade.

"You beat me just like Robin Hood!"

Napoleon laughed. "Yes, but there's more to learn!"

He taught Joe lines of defense and the ten parries of Olympic fencing. He also demonstrated a complex saber defense to use against a parry-quinte attack. The goal of which was to make contact with the opponent's blade, so it put his weapon just off the center line.

"We will continue to practice these moves and fence with each other so that the techniques become virtually ingrained within you, like instinct," Napoleon explained. He showed a swift contre-tierce and a fluid beat-parry-riposte. "With the quick riposte, you can break your opponent's blade. When this happens, you will know you have mastered the art of fencing!"

Joe and Napoleon continued to practice while Rose played a masterpiece with beautiful precision. Joe was inspired by the style and artistry with which she played Rodrigo's music. Her style was therapeutic for the mind and soul.

Rose's music renewed his energy and inspired Joe. He shouted, "I will win this match!"

Napoleon remembered back to the Olympic Games and his final match, when his German opponent had shouted something vulgar to him about the French people. Those words penetrated Napoleon's subconscious and distracted him, losing him the gold medal.

He brought his mind back to the present, crying, "Vive la France! Not this time!"

He ran hard at Joe used an extension then lunged at Joe, but Joe remained calm and used nimble footwork to retreat. He responded to Napoleon's every move like an echo, defending himself from everything Napoleon threw at him. Napoleon used Olympic style to attack at Joe's lines of defense—the sixte high outside line, the quarte high inside line, the octave low outside line, and the septime low inside line—but Joe did powerful parries followed by a riposte that did not touch. The experienced Napoleon used different footwork speeds when attacking Joe for strategy. He had attacked Joe with tempo speeds that were slow, medium, or explosively fast. In fencing, this tactic makes it difficult for the opponent to get the fencers timing down. Consequently, Joe finds it difficult to attack Napoleon. Joe places his sword out in an extension, but Napoleon continues to confuse Joe's timing, so he cannot do a riposte, or an attack after he parries an attack from Napoleon. Both fencers are doing a chess game in fencing, enhancing the thrill of the sport.

Suddenly, Herbie flew into Napoleon's eyes. Joe immediately attacked, lunging with his sword and using a faux pas to gain distance. Joe nearly struck Napoleon, but lucky Napoleon slipped and fell to the ground. Joe thinks to himself that Napoleon must have won the silver medal with skill and luck. Then Joe improvises and comes up with an idea. Joe advances and pushes off with his back foot for a powerful lunge at Napoleon. The athletic boy lets his back foot come off the ground, so his balance is completely on his front foot to get an extra lean forward for a final, match-winning point.

Herbie flapped in circles around them and squawked, "Joe wins! Joe wins!"

They all smiled and laughed with delight. Joe saluted his maestro with the sword as Napoleon returned one to his student. Then they shook hands to conclude the formal etiquette in Olympic swordplay fencing. Napoleon was humbled with honor to teach Joe new swordplay knowledge, and had pride as a maestro knowing his student improvised to acquire a win. Joe was extremely grateful to add more technique to his already samurai swordsmanship skills. Joe felt growing omnipotent in swordplay, with a great maestro such as Napoleon, to polish his skills. He knew it was the Zen way of life to thirst for new knowledge and to continually seek to improve oneself. Every new day presented an opportunity.

24

One early Saturday morning, the Benson family arrived at church.

"Why do we always go to church on Saturdays and not Sundays?" Joe asked.

"To recognize the true Sabbath Day, which is the seventh day of the week. It was set apart by God as a time of rest and spiritual rejuvenation. It is written in the Holy Bible, Matthew 28:1, that the Sabbath is the end of the week, and Sunday is the first day of the week. This alone is evidence, proof from the Ancient written Scriptures identifying the true Sabbath day. I know other people go to church on other days, and that's fine, as long as you know the true Sabbath day. The Sabbath day was made to benefit man—to remember he has a creator!" General Benson explained. "The people in the world are confused by the devil, and that's what Satan wants, confusion about the laws of God! Let me tell you something. Unfortunately, that exists in some churches, too, children. Regarding churches I learned many years ago, from an army chaplain captain, who said, 'Seek the powerful gift God gave you, and not indulge with people in idle gossip while you seek to judge others—but to seek God!'"

"Grandfather, how do we know that God exists?" Rose asked.

"For one thing, the US government prints the motto 'In God We Trust' on all American money. That's good enough for me. I worked for the government all my life, in the military, and I'm proud of it! Jesus himself said, 'The kingdom of God is within you.' So you see, Joe and Rose, God is a sort of energy of goodness. You can feel God's presence. No one can see God in his true form, but we can feel him in spirit."

Joe remembered his father saying the same thing his grandfather had just said.

"Are you trying to tell me to trust in God always?" Joe reflected.

"Yes, Joe. If you do, then you will be following the Golden Rule, doing unto others as you would have them do unto you."

"We will always trust in God," the children both promised. "And we will always follow the Golden Rule."

The general hugged his caring family, and they hugged him back.

"Gentlemen, please excuse me," Rose said. "I see the priest signaling me to take my place at the church organ."

"Play like the beautiful Rose we know, pretty angel!" the general said.

"Yes, go play, sister," Joe seconded. "Your style of playing always gives me peace eternal."

Everyone felt warm and happy listening to Rose play inspirational religious music on the huge church pipe organ. Mysteriously though, Joe's sixth sense kicked in as he saw a few evil-looking people with bad demeanors suddenly get up and depart the church eye-balling Joe.

The priest sprinkled everyone with holy water and gave a parting homily. "I know mass can be long at sometimes, and I appreciate everyone that stayed for the entire mass. I see who you are as I look around, for this is proof of your tolerance and faith in God, and I am honored to be in your presence! Bring honor into the world every day by always using honorable words. Carry yourself with honor wherever you go, and people around you will feel honored by your presence. In closing, remember the fifth commandment, 'Honor your father, and your mother!' Appreciate them while they are with you in the living. Believe in God, for God believes in you! Mass is over. Go in peace!"

Many people smiled and shook each other's hands, but Joe and Rose cried remembering their father and mother. Their grandfather, General Benson, comforted his grandchildren and said, "I am with you Joe and Rose. And I love you both, don't worry." The Bensons left the church as General Benson gave the Catholic priest an unusual hand sign, which the priest acknowledged as he smiled in harmony.

25

Years passed, and Joe was now a young man. It was time for him to learn a very important martial art lesson—the art of dying. Sensei Musashi had been taking Joe to the bad neighborhoods of Los Angeles once a week, where gangs and other criminals lived.

On the first time, they had gone into LA in a rental car. Sensei drove down into a dangerous-looking barrio and said, "Yes! This is a place where you will find some nice young Mexican American people to talk to." He let Joe out and promised to come back after returning the rental car.

Joe began walking. He came across a low-rider exhibit and entered. Suddenly, four beautiful Chicana models swarmed around him and asked him if he wanted a ride. Joe sensed something was up, but he knew he was there to learn a lesson. He didn't see sensei anywhere, so he said, "Sure!" The beautiful Latina bikini models took Joe in one of the low-rider cars to a bad area.

The car stopped. About ten Chicano gang members walked up to the car and yelled at Joe.

"Get out of the car, white boy, so we can kill you! But tell us first, how much money do you have? Comprende, cabrón?"

"Primero, let's have fun with him!" the models said.

"Sí, let's have mucho fun first!" the leader of the gang agreed. By now, most of the gang members were pointing guns at Joe. He felt death in the air, possibly his death. Adrenaline surged in his bloodstream.

"Fun," he said. "Yes, let's have fun. But I don't have any money."

"Then take off your shirt so that I can see you're not wired, ese," said the leader. Joe took off his shirt— revealing his chest muscles, six-pack abs, and bulging forearms, biceps, and shoulders. Everyone noticed Joe's muscular figure. The bikini models whistled.

"Hey, he works out a lot!" said some of the gang members.

"I tell you what," the leader said to Joe. "If you can beat up Macho here, then you can walk out of here alive." A huge man appeared from behind a door. He looked to be about 6 feet 9 inches tall with 350 pounds of solid muscle. Macho took off his shirt, displaying a tattoo across his chest that read "Macho."

Joe put himself into a Zen trance and felt for his sixth sense as he awaited Macho's oncoming attack. Joe knew that his fancy martial art skills would not work in this situation; he knew he would have to feel what to do without planning. Joe did not want to go to the ground with Macho either; there were other gang members that could possibly jump in to attack him.

The gang leader said, "Crush him, Macho!"

Macho tried to grab Joe, but Joe felt his energy coming and tripped him. Macho fell to the ground, hard. The onlookers passed around some popcorn while they watched the fight. "Orale, hombre!" Macho got up and grabbed for Joe again. This time, he succeeded in catching him, but Joe grabbed him back, locking onto his energy. Each man was trying to overpower the other. The muscles of their abs, chests, and arms strained in a deadlock.

Macho quickly grew tired, but Joe did not. He used a martial arts technique called body connection. Joe, after many years of honing this skill, can feel a person's moves before they move by connecting to them. Joe turned Macho around using Macho's own energy against him. Then Joe used his hip to easily guide Macho into a chair.

"Please, Macho, sit! I wish you no harm!" Joe said. He followed the same statement in Spanish to comfort Macho since Joe was fluent in Spanish. "Les deseo ninguno dano señor!"

"Muy bien. Very good," the gang leader said. "You, Joe, have honor. It seems that God has shined on you today. You may leave with your life. Adiós!"

"Hasta la vista," Joe said. He put his shirt back on and walked away.

He found himself in a bad neighborhood. Cars zoomed by blasting music, dogs were running loose everywhere, and the walls and streets were all covered with graffiti.

A low-rider car pulled up next to Joe. Someone inside said, "Do you need a lift, amigo?"

Joe peered inside and saw none other than Sensei Musashi, smiling.

Joe laughed. "Yes, please, give me a ride! I will buy lunch!"

They stopped at a family taco stand two blocks away.

"Here?" Joe asked.

"Here, Joe!" Sensei said.

They went in and ate delicious tacos with salsa and drank horchata, rice water with fresh cinnamon. Many Latinos were eating there.

One young man said to Sensei, "Hey, viejo! Nice ride you got there."

"Gracias, joven! I like my car too. It's rad!"

"You sure speak good Spanish, Sensei," Joe said.

"Yes, I do, because I'm old. But who taught you, Joe? Your Spanish is excelente."

"Lumbra taught me when I was a child. She taught me many things from her culture. I had to speak good Spanish or I got no French pastries from Napoleon. Now I'm glad I learned to speak fluently, para ser caballero. But Sensei, what's with your car?"

"A true martial artist is able to blend into any environment. This is the 'way' to stay out of trouble." They laughed together as they continued to enjoy their good Mexican food. They struck up conversations in Spanish with the other diners. It was a friendly atmosphere.

Joe's face turned a little red when he ate the spicy chiles in his tacos. "Esta salsa esta muy picosa!"

Sensei laughed and told Joe that it was also part of the samurai way to enjoy the moment. "Eat more chilies, Joe!" Sensei exclaimed as he grabbed a big chile and ate it.

—⋙—

The following week, Sensei took Joe to a dangerous and unpredictable gang area in Oakland, California. This time he drove a nice, tricked-out car.

He spotted what he seemed to be looking for and said, "Yes, this is the place. There are some nice, young, African-American men around here. Good people!" He dropped Joe off. Joe walked through a pack of wild dogs harmless while he chomped on pistachios. As Joe walked, he stopped before attempting to walk around a middle-aged African-American man sitting on the curb, wearing a dusty battle dress uniform from the United States Army.

"Excuse me, may I walk around you, sir?" Joe says.

The man with a look of a warrior in his eyes, began to laugh at Joe then said "You're a civilian!"

Joe smiled. "Yes, my name is Joe Benson, but my grandfather is not a civilian."

"Benson? Not General Arnold Benson?" the army veteran said.

"Yes! That's my grandfather. Do you know him?" Joe says.

"I've been to war with the general. He's a good man! Name's Kibuka! But you're out of place in this area. You shouldn't be here young man," the veteran asserted.

"But Mr. Kibuka, why are you here, sir? This area of Oakland is a bad area. You're a military veteran that could be taken care of by the government."

"Why are you here, Joe? The government forgot all about me. Every time I tried to file a claim for veteran's compensation, my paper work got lost or I was denied. Anyhow, this place ain't nothing compared to what I've been in. There's no danger for me here. I still pack my .45 pistol from the war, and my survival knife's in my boot, just a reach away. Ain't nobody messing with me!"

"I'm here to learn a lesson, as my Sensei says. I trust my Sensei—he's like a father to me. But here is my phone number. I will ask my grandfather to help you, and I know he will." Joe hands Kibuka a paper with his phone number and a few dollars.

"No charity!" Kibuka gives back Joe his money but keeps the phone number. "But I would like to talk to the general. I walk around here all night and all day, just remembering the war, and the things I had to do! I feel like I just want it to all end, you know?"

"Take care, Kibuka!" Joe says as he offers the veteran his hand, but the veteran does not put his hand out, so Joe just walks slowly away.

"You! Take care, Joe!" the tough military veteran Kibuka says. As Joe walks away, Kibuka takes a higher ground, a house roof, to keep a visual on Joe.

Joe passed some gang members wearing Raiders hats and jerseys and gold chains. He thought to himself, *This is insane!*

One of them said, "Hey, bro, did you say insane? What's your white honky ass doing around here?"

The gang members circled Joe. Some of them opened up their jackets to show that they had guns. Trapped, Joe again felt the fear of death. His adrenaline kicked in—he had to decide to fight or flight.

"I mean no one harm," he insisted. They all laughed.

"Sh——t, your flagging that green lettuce to that crazy veteran. I'm gonna kick your ass, white boy!" one of the gang members said.

He swung his bare fists menacingly at Joe. Joe used his elbows effortlessly to deflect and defused the man's blows, which neutralize his energy. The man continued to pummel Joe very aggressively, but he quickly grew tired. He then lunged for Joe's neck, but Joe countered and raised his shoulders, lowering his head and neck deep inside his body, thus leaving no neck for the assailant to choke. This is called the turtle technique. Joe quickly used his hands to feel for the gang member's energy and connected to it then redirected the assailants attacking energy and spun him to the ground hard.

"Uuh!" The gang member cried. But with determined anger the young man got up and charged Joe again.

"You are tired! You should sleep!" Joe yelled then put the gang member in a jujitsu cross-arm rear neck choke. "Beddy-bye time!"

The man struggled to speak feeling his neck and jaw bone crushing. "No beddy-bye! Please, no beddy-bye! I don't like beddy-bye time!"

"I don't like beddy-bye time, either. Never have." Joe released him.

He still felt that he was in danger, but he didn't have that fight-or-flight impulse anymore. The gang leader pulled out his gun and showed it to Joe.

Joe accepted that he might die. He looked the gang leader in the eye, confident that it would take more than one bullet to kill him. *Shoot me*, Joe thought. *You'd better watch out, though, because I'll come right at you!*

But instead of firing, the leader handed off his gun to another gang member and started demonstrating to Joe some real street breakdancing. "Can you do that, G?"

"No way!" Joe admitted. "You're too good. But I can do this." He did a cartwheel, jumped high in the air, spun around three times like a ballet dancer, and landed on one hand.

The gang leader laughed. "You know, you're a person of honor. I can feel it! You're cool, bro. Can you teach me some of that crazy dance and kung fu sh——t?"

"It would be an honor to teach you some martial arts, but I'm not a good dancer. My mother was." Joe remembered Olivia's artistic ballet. "And my name is Joe."

"Okay, Cool Joe, show us what you know," he said.

Joe shared several martial arts lessons that he had learned from Sensei. According to Sensei, teaching martial arts or any constructive knowledge was a way to peace eternal. Before long, the young man who had attacked Joe apologized. Joe accepted the apology with honor.

Then the gang leader gave Joe his Raiders cap and said, "This is yours, Cool Joe. Thanks! Peace out!"

The gang walked away. Joe put the Raiders cap on and waved good-bye to his new friends.

Suddenly a tricked-out car stopped next to Joe, and the person inside asked, "You want to shake the spot?"

"Sure, Sensei. I'll buy you lunch. Let's go!" Joe said with a comforting feeling he's going to leave the area.

"You said it!" Sensei Musashi says.

They drove two blocks and stopped at a restaurant called Mama's Place.

"Eat here, Sensei?" Joe ponders.

"Yes! I'm hungry, and you invited me. Let's eat."

Sensei Musashi bows before he enters then walks in as if he's been here before. Joe follows his sensei as they sat down to buttermilk biscuits with fresh gravy. There were hunks of freshly steamed skinless chicken and vegetables mixed into the gravy. Sensei washed the delicious food down with a straight glass of buttermilk.

"Try it," he said. "They make it here."

"I don't like buttermilk. I tried drinking a store brand once. It sucks. I barfed it up."

The owner of the restaurant, a large African-American woman from the South, looked over toward their table. It was Mama herself. She had been brought up in the tradition of Southern hospitality and charm. She gestured to her daughter—a very attractive, full-figured young woman.

"Go see what's going on over there, sugar!" she said.

The daughter made her way over to their table. Joe was still refusing to drink the buttermilk. When he saw her, his eyes lit up. He stood up and said, "Would you like to sit with us? You're beautiful!"

Did I just say that out loud? he asked himself.

"I will sit with you, handsome, but only if you drink your buttermilk," Mama's daughter says.

"I promise!" Joe says. Mama's daughter sat next to Joe as he sees the military veteran Kibuka walk into the restaurant. Joe waves to Kibuka, and Kibuka points his index finger at Joe and smiles as he sits down at the bar stools next to Mama. Joe asks her if he could pay the tab for the veteran who just sat next to her mother.

"Oh no! He's our friend that comes and goes. He's here early today, as if he followed someone here?"

Mama's daughter and Joe talked about things they enjoy in life as they drank cold buttermilk on a hot summer day.

"This is buttermilk? This is delicious!" Joe exclaimed.

Sensei and the pretty young lady laughed.

"I told you Joe, drink it, drink the buttermilk!" said Sensei.

———

Another week went by. Sensei took Joe to a bad area in the Asian section of Los Angeles.

"This looks like a good place," he said. "You will find some nice young Asian American people around here, especially the young men. Good people. And remember, Joe, I taught you some of the Chinese language too. A good samurai should blend into any Asian community." He dropped Joe off again then drove away. Joe knows fluent Japanese and good basic Chinese language—thanks to Sensei.

Joe couldn't see anything good. To him, it just looked like a not-so-good area. He was hungry, so he went into an Asian restaurant. He ate a huge meal, but he had to swat flies away the whole time on the hot summer night. He ordered two more plates of food. A gorgeous, full-figured Asian waitress brought his order to him then smiled as she walked away.

Four Asian gang members walked in and gave Joe the evil eye. Joe suspected they were members of the infamous gang known as the Flies. One of them came close and pulled out a knife, looking at Joe to see if he was afraid. Once again, Joe felt death in the air and adrenaline pumped into his body. Would he fight or run? He seemed to be getting used to having to make this decision. Sensei said it was the experience a martial artist needed; becoming comfortable with conflict was part of the way. Only a true martial arts sensei would guide someone through this much-needed lesson, he knew.

Joe was getting used to controlling his fear and beginning to understand that death and life were one.

Instead of responding in a predictable way, he decided to surprise his adversary with a display of wit. With his chopsticks, he grabbed four flies out of the air and put them close to his open mouth, as if to eat them.

"But wait," he said. "These four are innocent. But I really don't know about the other four in here." He winked at the beautiful young Asian waitress then released the flies back into the air.

The attractive young lady laughed, in awe of Joe's quick reflexes and humor. The four gang members called Flies were not amused. One of them was clearly jealous that Joe was flirting with the pretty young waitress. In the Asian community, the "Flies" were known to pester people, and to "fly" through the air with their good fighting skills. The Flies' core martial art foundation is wushu kung fu.

Suddenly one of the young men shoved his knife right in Joe's face. Joe intercepted his energy, though, and slammed him onto the table that held two full plates of food.

"Tastes good, huh?" Joe said.

The restaurant's owner shouted for all of them to go outside and settle their argument there.

"Let's go outside, *bairen nanhai*. You think you're a Chinese shaolin kung fu master or a Japanese samurai, huh?" the gang member asked as he grabbed paper towels to clean himself up with.

Outside, the gang member angrily wiped Joe's food off his face. Everyone inside the restaurant was looking out the windows. They could see that Joe gave off an aura of assuredness. Joe felt in control. He had no fear. Nevertheless, the gang member said, "You don't know Chinese boxing, or Gung Fu—so I am going to teach you!"

Calm down. Relax! Breathe air! Joe told himself.

The gang member allowed his anger to control his emotions. He jumped high in the air then spun in an attempt to strike Joe in the temple with the heel of his foot. Joe responded like an echo to safely back away from kicking range as soon as he recognized that the Asian gangster's telegraphed kick. The gang member became furious.

"Don't move, *bairen nanhai!*" he shouted. The gang member did a sliding side kick at Joe, but Joe fluidly parried it with his hand out of center line, escaping any harm.

He rushed Joe, attempting to take him to the ground, so his buddies can jump in on top of Joe. But Joe knew this, and he leapt over the Asian gangster while grabbing his collar, choking the gang member with his own shirt. Joe continued to tighten the Asia gangster's shirt, pressing into the carotid while keeping a watchful eye on the other gang members. The young Asian under Joe's masterful submission was helpless—began to black out—then took a submissive pose.

The young Asian gang member gasped as if it were his last breathe—and he fearfully said in Chinese, "*Tingzhi. Wo buneng huxi!* (Stop. I can't breathe!)"

"*Qing huxi!* (Please breathe!)" Joe responded, releasing him. "I mean you no harm."

"How do you know the Chinese language?" the young man asked in English.

"Believe it or not, I'm Chinese."

The four young men looked at Joe's very Caucasian face and then laughed. "Not!" they said.

They shook hands with Joe, said they were sorry about everything, and told Joe his presence brought honor to the Asian community.

"You're no white devil. You're a man of honor. We can feel your chi spirit energy," they said as they walked away.

A car pulled up next to him, and the person inside said in Japanese, "*Bushi no josha ga hitsuyodesu ka?* (Need a ride, samurai?)"

Joe got in as usual but did not say anything.

"Are you hungry, Joe?" Sensei asked.

Joe was a little bit hungry since he hadn't gotten to finish his last two plates of food, but he decided he wasn't going to be tricked again into staying in a bad neighborhood for a meal. So he said, "I'm not hungry, Sensei. Just thirsty."

"Well, now I'm thirsty too!" Sensei drove two more blocks and pulled up in front of a Japanese restaurant. "Let's go inside and quench our thirst!"

Joe knew he was up to something. He wasn't biting. "Sure, let's drink. Promise me, though, no eating any cooked food."

"I promise, Joe. No cooked food."

Inside the restaurant, they drank a lot of sake while beautiful young geishas danced and sang for them.

"This sushi is delicious," Joe said. "And it's not cooked!"

They drank some more. Sensei put a huge bowl of fish eyes on the table. "Eat these, Joe! They taste like grapes. Our agreement was that food may not be cooked, right?"

"Okay," Joe said bravely. "I like grapes." He put a huge handful of fish eyes into his mouth and started chomping. "Yep, taste like grapes!"

The fish eyes burst in Joe's mouth. Some fluid leaked out the side of his mouth and dripped down his face and neck.

Sensei Musashi laughed hard and took a handful too. "Yes. Eat more grapes, Joe!"

They laughed and went on eating sushi and grape-flavored fish eyes and drinking sake all night long. Joe felt happy while he listened to Sensei's old samurai stories.

—⁓—

A week later, Sensei Musashi came to pick up Joe at the Benson house as usual.

"How did you learn to control your fear of death?" he asked. "Could you go now into battle knowing you might die?"

"Life and death are one," Joe answered. "I now accept that I might die. These experiences you have given me have enlightened me to live life in this way, Sensei."

Sensei Musashi was pleased. He decided to take Joe on one more life-or-death trip.

For this last trip, they went all the way to a poor "white" rural town in Texas.

"This is the place," Sensei said. "There are a lot of tough people around here, so be careful! Try to blend in this time, like a true martial artist."

"But I'm Caucasian! How could I not blend in? What will the lesson be, Sensei?"

Sensei Musashi just laughed and drove off into the sunset.

Joe walked along the side of the road. Soon a pickup truck stopped and the man inside asked, "Need a lift, partner?"

Joe's gut instinct told him this was a violent man who should be avoided. "No thank you, sir!"

"Suit yourself, dipsh——t," the man grumbled and then peeled away fast.

Next, three beautiful country girls in blue jeans pulled up in a convertible. They stood up and asked, "Need a lift, cowboy?"

"Where are you ladies going?"

The driver—an attractive, full-figured blonde girl—said, "We're going to the rodeo dance. How about you?"

"I would be honored to dance with all of you." He squeezed in. The girls didn't mind being pressed up next to handsome young Joe.

At the dance, they showed him how to do the two-step. Joe picked up the moves quickly and showed off the athleticism he inherited from his ballerina mother.

A few feet away, the large Texan that had offered Joe a ride was having a conversation with a few cowboys. The rowdy big cowboys asked the big Texan if he wanted a drink of beer.

The big Texan declined, saying, "I'm a big game hunter. I don't drink liquor. I've skinned bears, mountain lions, and wild boar. You name it, I've skinned it."

The cowboys laughed. They drank more beer and said, "Hey, big hunter. You're good with animals, but not good with women!" The cowboys continued to rile the big hunter, saying, "Hey, look hunter, that pretty boy is no cowboy, and he's got three of our Texas womenfolk!"

The big Texan hunter looked over and saw Joe with the three beautiful young ladies. He recognized him as the hitchhiker.

"I remember that dipsh——t," he said to the others. "He thinks he's too good to ride with me, and now he's bothering our womenfolk!"

The cowboys laughed and said, "Yeah, he's bothering our womenfolk. Go get him big game hunter!"

The hunter took out a big, sharp hunting knife and began to stalk Joe like he was prey.

Joe stopped dancing with the lovely young ladies when he sensed danger. He whirled around just in time to see the big man from the pickup truck attempting to stick him in the ribs with a hunting knife. Joe knew it was fight-or-flight time; his previous experiences allowed him to concentrate fully now. He intercepted the big hunter's forearm while simultaneously striking the hand that held the hunting knife. The knife clattered to the floor. He moved the big hunter's body toward his own.

"Kia!" Joe shouted and smashed the big game hunter's face with his elbow, which exploded with blood in the air. People moved out of the way, but some got showered with the hunter's blood. Joe followed with a hip throw that sent the big cowboy to the ground so hard the dance floor rumbled.

All the cowboys laughed and said, "Well, doggies!"

A group of four Texas Rangers appeared immediately. They quickly escorted the big game hunter away from the dance.

One Ranger laughed and said to Joe, "Don't worry, young man. We saw the whole thing. You didn't start the fight. We'd have stopped it sooner, but we couldn't get to him before he started attacking you."

"Excuse me, Mr. Ranger, but why do you think he attacked me in the first place?"

"That's the cowboy way of life, young man. And your night's not over yet!" He winked at the three beautiful young ladies who had slung their arms around Joe.

"Hey, handsome, you have a body on you," one of the girls said, peering at his pectoral muscles and ripped abs through his badly torn shirt.

"You've got some blood on your clothes, cowboy. You need to get cleaned up!" another girl said. "How about coming to our house so you can put on one of my brother's shirts?"

Joe recognized how dirty he was. His shirt was beyond repair. "All right. Seeing as I'm practically not wearing a shirt anymore, yes, I could use another. But I will pay you ladies for it!"

The girls looked at each other and laughed. "Let's go, tough cowboy. We country girls will take real good care of you!"

They took him outside. They all squeezed back into the convertible.

Soon, they pulled up to a big ranch home with a lot of open space. There were no neighbors, just cattle and horses wandering around a paddock.

Joe's sixth sense told him this was nice country living. "Where's your brother?" he asked. The girls just laughed and escorted him inside.

"How about some lemonade?" one of the girls asked. "We also got homemade ice cream. It's a hot summer night."

Joe and the girls got cleaned up. Once Joe had put on a fresh shirt, all four of them sat outside on a huge front porch to take in the fresh air. The girls giggled as they saw Joe gulp down two tall glasses of fresh, cold, sweet lemonade. Then they ate ice cream and talked.

Joe spotted a guitar on the porch. "Nice guitar."

"It's our brother's. He's not coming back till tomorrow. Can you play?"

He took a drink of some of their cool homemade lemonade. "I know a little." He picked up the guitar and began to play, singing a nice country tune. After a while, the four of them fell asleep together on a huge bench on the porch.

Joe woke up in the morning to find himself surrounded by the three beautiful Texan girls. They were still on the front porch. A big pickup truck approached the house. Joe assumed it was probably the brother, but when the truck stopped, Sensei Musashi stepped out.

"Hello, Joe! Ready to head back to California?"

"I'm hungry, Sensei," he said, reluctant to leave the arms of the three beautiful girls. They began to wake. Overhearing the talk of food, one suggested, "Let's have a big, ranch-style breakfast!"

"Where should we go?" Joe asked.

Just then, another truck approached the house. This time it was the girls' brother and father.

"What's going on around here?" the father asked.

"Hey, Pa. This is Joe," one girl said. "He can dance, fight, play guitar, and sing good. And he's not married!"

The other girls laughed. Joe stood up, held out his hand, and said, "I'm Joe. It's a pleasure to meet you, sir."

The father saw a handsome, athletic-looking young man standing before him and thought Joe might make just a good son-in-law and a good ranch hand rolled into one.

"Hello, young man!" he said. "My name is Ethan. You're staying for breakfast. My daughter, Olivia, is the best cook in Texas. She can also ride a horse like the wind."

"Your daughter's name is Olivia?" Joe was suddenly flooded with sadness.

Sensei felt his sorrow. "History repeats itself sometimes, Joe. This is the way of man. But Joe, Bushido will help you on your life's journey." Joe feels he excels at everything, but still has not found his peace eternal.

"Thanks, Sensei! I always learn many lessons from you. And how to eat was one of them!"

Sensei laughed and slapped Joe lightly on the back since he feels Joe has not yet found his peace eternal.

As they all walked in to eat a country-style breakfast, the brother looked at Joe. "Hey! He's wearing my shirt, Pa!"

"That shirt never looked good on you anyway, so pipe down!" said the father.

"It sure looks great on Joe!" Olivia said.

They all enjoyed Olivia's country cooking. She made them steak, eggs, potatoes, gravy, biscuits, and, most importantly, served them fresh, raw cow milk to wash it all down.

"Drink the milk, Joe!" Sensei said, teasing him. Joe happily drank all the milk and asked for more.

26

On a fine warm Sunday afternoon, Joe, Rose, General Benson, Lumbra, and Napoleon were at a beach in Santa Monica. Joe caught some nice waves on his surfboard, while Rose and the general watched. Lumbra and Napoleon were preparing a salad of mixed greens, sunflower seeds, and French bread rolls he had baked fresh at the Benson house early that morning. Lumbra also placed cut-up fruit in small bowls to be served after the main meal. Napoleon enjoyed preparing meals with Lumbra close by his side. He thought her curvy Latina body looked beautiful in a bikini, but he was even more attracted to the gorgeous face that went along with her intelligent, scientific mind.

"Lumbra, ma chérie, the meal, my masterpiece, is ready," Napoleon said. "Please call the Bensons to come eat!"

She kissed him and then trotted away to speak to the Bensons. As she walked, the heads of young and old men alike turned to watch her. She quickly found Rose and the general. It seemed that Joe had attracted a crowd; people were in awe of his surfing skills. He had been doing flips on the board while riding the waves.

Rose, who was also in a bikini and looked like a supermodel, called, "Joe, stop showing off! You're just like Mom."

"He does have that entertaining gene, but so do you, Rose," her grandfather reminded her. "You are probably the best pianist in the world. You are both special."

Rose and Lumbra jumped up and down in an attempt to get Joe's attention, but he didn't see them.

General Benson shouted, "Enough of this! Hey, Joe! Napoleon's meal is ready!"

Joe's ears caught Napoleon's name. "I'm coming! Tengo mucho hambre! Save some for me!" He raced out of the water with his surfboard. All the young ladies nearby watched him.

Napoleon served his salad masterpiece with the fresh rolls and said, "Bon appétit!" He slapped his mouth with his hand to make his trademark popping sound. Everyone laughed, including some onlookers. Napoleon and Lumbra romantically bit from the same roll in unison. The Bensons were enjoying each others' company. They were a happy family. Napoleon noticed that Joe had brought his guitar, not just his surfboard, to the beach.

When they had finished eating, Napoleon asked, "Joe, since I taught you how to speak my beautiful French language, will you play something on your guitar for Lumbra and me?"

Joe was grateful to have learned the lovely French language from a native speaker, so he obliged. "Mais oui! Ah, amour." Joe played a beautiful song by Joaquín Rodrigo while Rose sang the words. The entire beach seemed to be in a state of peace eternal.

27

Several years went by, and Joe practiced the way every day by living according to the samurai code of conduct. One morning, Joe was wearing his hakama pants and sitting on the gym floor in front of a large picture window that overlooked his late mother's garden. He breathed calmly in deep meditation as he gazed at the eye-pleasing garden of Olivia—a reminder of his mother's elegance—and felt at peace.

Joe knew that when a person was awake, his conscious mind was active; and when a person was asleep, his subconscious mind was active. That was why he practiced deep meditation every morning, to clear both his conscious and subconscious mind. He listened to himself breathing to relax without daydreaming. He focused on just inhaling good oxygen. This form of meditation was taught to him by Sensei Musashi and was based on samurai Zen practice. He followed this routine every morning to recharge his battery, so to speak. It gave him energy to start a new day. Meditation also helped develop his chi energy. Joe believed in God, and he also believed that chi was a form of divine power given to him for constructive use. Through years of training and personal guidance by Sensei Musashi, Joe had reached the highest level of chi within himself. In a confrontation, he now also had the ability to control his attacker's chi. If a person committed himself to a course of action, he was also committing his chi. Joe understood this now.

He came out of his meditative state by slowly opening his eyes. Once Joe had come completely back into the present, he noticed that his mind and body felt supercharged with energy. It had been a perfect meditation session that morning.

Joe suddenly felt his sensei's presence. There was a light knock at the gym door, and then Sensei Musashi entered.

"Ohayo gozaimasu, Joe! Your grandfather said I could find you in here. Are you ready?"

"Good morning to you, too, Sensei. Sashiburi (Long time no see)!" Joe did a formal rei as he bowed to his teacher. According to Sensei Musashi, Joe had shown honor by learning the Japanese language, which he believed all samurai should know.

"Joe, it has been an honor to teach you martial arts for all these years in the old way. You know, it was your father who requested that I teach you the way of the samurai. Dr. Benson honored my family when he cured me and my family members of osteoporosis and Parkinson's disease. He also cured me of cancer shortly before he went to the other world. It's tragic that when your father died, he took all his secret cures with him!"

"Yes. I will always love my father and mother. I feel them with me every day."

"This is because you have reached the highest level of chi energy and are now connected to the energy that exists all around us."

For that day's lesson, Sensei reviewed all the various types of swords, including medieval broadswords, military swords such as cavalry swords, modern swords, Japanese swords, and holy swords such as the one said to be wielded by Michael the Archangel. Joe was already so knowledgeable about sword design that he could look at any sword or its inscription and tell for what purpose it had been made.

"Now, can you recite from memory the philosophy of a true swordsman, one who is master of all swords, Bushido, and the five ways of strategy?" Sensei asked.

"Bushido is the way of the warrior. My Bushido life will be a moral code of frugality, loyalty, martial arts mastery, and honor unto death. Ground strategy of having a good foundation in the area you are fighting and use things in the area against your opponent. Water strategy of being formless or shapeless by changing tactics while fighting fluidly, and both in fighting and everyday life should be determined through calm. Water strategy, you must act and not contemplate on a decision. Water strategy is to always keep flowing just as running water never goes stale. Do not allow bad criticism of you by friend, foe, or enemy to alter your calmness.

"Fire strategy of having fire, heat, sun light or any light to blind or burn your opponent while fighting. This strategy also works to gain advantage in a conversation. Wind strategy just as wind travels across the sea or land. A person must travel many lands to learn different cultures and many occupations for knowledge. This means a person must learn about his opponent or enemy to know their strengths and weakness. Void strategy is to have an open mind. Void is the knowledge you do not have. Void is the opponent, enemy, or area of the world you do not know. Void is not to fret about what you do not know, but knowing what you do know is enough. Void is to never have confrontation if there is another option. Do not fight if you can walk away. Do not argue with someone to convince them on matters when knowing is enough, for this is Bushido.

"A true master swordsman can wield any heavy or long sword in either hand and is able to pick up any sword in battle to use against the enemy. He is confident that he can use any sword thrust upon him skillfully while keeping his honor. A master swordsman is surrounded by an aura of good. This alone often deters any foes from picking fights with him. This aura also gives a master swordsman an unbeatable fighting spirit!"

"Good, Joe. Listen to this next lesson, which is the most important of all. I know you have heard this before, but etch it in your memory. When you make a mistake, ask what you can learn from it. This is the way. And trust your instincts! They are your sixth sense. They are divine power guiding you. So that you may learn these lessons, I have taken you to bad neighborhoods. Most of the people living there do not know the way. Some of them threatened to kill you. But, Joe, you accepted that death and life are one. You have had experiences where you feared that you might die, which initially prevented you from coordinating all your limbs in self-defense. They also allowed you to learn to know what works and what your limitations are. The actual experience of a fight-or-flight situation cannot be taught in any dojo. This is why you and I practice using real swords against each other. In using actual weapons, we take the chance of losing a limb, or even our lives. This is the authentic way of practicing martial arts. A real martial artist puts his life on the line and accepts that he may die. This liberates him so that he dies with honor."

"Yes, Sensei, I feel with my sixth sense that now I am liberated!" Joe exclaimed.

"Yes, that's it!" Sensei proudly said. "Your sixth sense, Joe! The highest level of self-knowledge is the ability to use your sixth sense whether you're a fighter or a businessman. This sixth sense, along with experience and practice in controlling your fear, will make you omnipotent. You will be able to achieve victory over any opponent. Use your sixth sense when making a decision crucial to your survival or success in life. Use it constantly, Joe, so that it becomes natural. This is the way!"

"I practice using my sixth sense every day, Sensei. For example, I felt your presence before you knocked on the gym door."

"Good! These strategies will help you throughout your lifetime in whatever you choose to do. They will also assist you on life's journey to the super form or life beyond!"

The pair donned their kendo equipment and began to practice. Their wooden swords struck each other with an almost musical rhythm. At times, as they picked up the pace, their swords made loud, fast noises and sounded more like machine guns. Joe glided across the floor like a gazelle. Suddenly, with artistry and grace, he thrust his wooden sword at Sensei Musashi, and succeeded in touching him lightly on the upper abdomen.

Sensei Musashi said, "Stop! Joe, you are extra special. You definitely inherited your mother's athleticism! Now it is time for your final test. We will use real Japanese swords. I know you like classical music, but I will throw you off by playing my music instead. Here!"

He handed Joe a tiny thumb drive of traditional Japanese music. Joe put the drive into a stereo system over near the piano. He liked to practice along to music from the stereo when his sister could not play the piano for him. He preferred to hear Rose play, of course, but not when Sensei Musashi was there to teach him. Sensei's private lessons were meant for Joe's ears only, and Joe honored his teacher's request.

"There is no other way to teach," Sensei Musashi would say.

Beautiful Japanese music echoed throughout the gym.

Sensei Musashi said, "Samurai Joe, show me ken-jutsu swordsmanship. Show me any swordsmanship knowledge you have. Show me your open mind! A true samurai can cut off two or more heads in battle with one graceful swing of his sword. Show me you know the way. Show me you are a samurai!"

Teacher and student used a broken rhythm to gain distance from each other. When they did clash, the real Japanese swords made metallic clangs ring throughout the room.

These attracted General Benson's attention.

"It must be a real good lesson. It reminds me of my days at West Point," General Benson said to himself as he sat in the study and puffed on a cigar to calm his nerves.

After a time, Sensei said, "Stop! Now close your eyes and use your sixth sense. You must harness this sense for use in combat and everywhere you go. You already have some experience in using it and have mastered your fear of dying. Remember that life and death are one when a person follows the way. I will not close my eyes, though, Joe, for I am old. If I am able to cut off one of your limbs, then you will know you are not yet a samurai."

Joe closed his eyes. He could feel the adrenaline starting to pump through his body. He knew the danger was real with those sharp swords. Even an accidental swing of the razor-sharp blades could cut off a head or arm. The actual battle began. As they sparred, Joe got cut on his forearm. Sensei saw Joe bleeding and knew what he had to do—he must go beyond just cutting his student. Sensei took a breath for energy. A look of complete determination came across his face. He swung his mighty sword and the unforeseen happened—Joe suddenly opened his eyes and intercepted Sensei's powerful sword with a technique called beat-parry-riposte. He channeled all his chi energy at the weapon. Sensei Musashi's sword broke in half, which made a sound like thunder in the sky.

"Stop, Joe! Good, my son! You are a master samurai! Your sixth sense guided you to victory!"

Proud tears slid down Joe's cheeks. "Forgive me, Sensei, for breaking your beautiful sword!"

"I am proud of you like a father is proud of his son. You broke an Ancient relic samurai sword that was designed to be humanly unbreakable. Yet you did it."

"What does it mean?"

"It means you know the way. You are meant to live forever!"

Joe contemplated this. "Sensei, after all these years, I feel like you are a father to me. Will I see you again?"

"No, Joe, you will not see me again. But you will always feel me with you in this life and in the one to come. And be careful, Joe! A person such as you knowing the true Bushido will be targeted by an evil power. This is part of the way!"

Joe smiled. "I feel like the way gives me a peace eternal from God."

"Yes! God! But you, Joe, are a samurai! You will have to face evil with or without a God at your side. Remember to always live by the way, and you will live in peace eternal and know harmony. When you want to see birds, look at them. If you want to hear music, then listen to music. If you want to make love to a woman, then make love to her. If you want to play with your children, then play with them. Do constructive things every day that help you. Remember that everything around you will improve for you if you improve yourself. I will not say good-bye, because I will always be with you. Remember that!"

"I'm hungry and thirsty, Sensei."

"Thirsty and hungry? Good! A samurai always thirsts and hungers for more knowledge. Always keep an open mind for new things! Now go out and eat and drink life itself!"

They bowed to each other in a show of mutual respect. Sensei Musashi left the room quietly. Joe watched him go with tears streaming down his face.

28

Joe's memories of his parents were quality ones. He would never forget his father. He had been a great physician and biologist. Neither would he forget his beautiful mother. Olivia Benson had been a great English ballerina who possessed extraordinary athleticism. She had a pleasant personality and had adoring fans all over the world. Although Joe found comfort in having his grandfather and sister living with him, he still missed his parents.

While in the gym one day, Joe heard Herbie laughing. Through the large picture window, he saw the bird fly softly into the garden. Joe went outside without his shirt on. He could feel the warm sun upon his body. Herbie landed on his left shoulder, and the pair strolled through the garden full of flowers and rare plants. He stopped and thought awhile. He had his eyes closed, and he listened to the fish in their pond and to the buzzing of the insects and hummingbirds. He inhaled the scent of the flowers and plants.

"This area of the garden smells like my mother," he said to Herbie. "I can remember my father carrying me on his shoulders here. Now I carry you on my shoulders, Herbie!"

"Joe! Joe! Look!"

He opened his eyes in time to see Herbie jump into some rose bushes. Then he spotted something under the bird's feet.

Herbie grabbed a small volcanic rock with his toes and squawked. "Doctor Robert! Doctor Robert!"

"What do you mean, Herbie? What about my father?" He reached down and picked the rock up off the ground. There, below the rock, he could see a metal object. Joe scraped some soil away. It soon became evident that he was uncovering a metal safe.

"Doctor Robert! Doctor Robert!" Herbie repeated again.

"Are you telling me this safe belonged to my father?" Joe asked the bird.

Herbie bobbed his head to indicate yes. Joe took the small safe to the study for privacy. Herbie had reclaimed his perch on his left shoulder. Joe examined the metal box. It was a combination safe made of titanium. A message was engraved on it.

> To my son, Joe: Speak the correct answer for these three questions and the voice-activated combination lock will open. I always had confidence and faith that somehow you would find this safe. It is meant only for you. If someone else tries to open it and fails, an acid capsule inside will break, destroying all the contents.

Question one read, "What is my son's favorite movie?"

"Robin Hood!" Joe said. He heard a click as the voice-activated lock moved.

Question two read, "What is my dear wife, Olivia's, favorite flower?"

"A rose!" he said excitedly. The lock moved again.

The third question read, "How did Joe's parents come up with his name?"

Joe knew that coffee had been his parents' favorite drink, and that they called it a cup of joe. That had to be the answer. He said confidently, "Coffee!"

The safe made a final, loud click and sprung open. He had answered all three questions correctly. Inside the safe, he discovered liquid medication sealed in special airtight vials. They were labeled "Cancer Cure." There were also some unused syringes and papers covered with mathematical formulas. He saw a second label on an envelope that read "Cancer cure formula with required diet and exercise regime." There was also a small disk, labeled "Message to surviving family."

Joe took the disk to the study. He sat still for a moment, calming himself by engaging in a brief meditation session. After a few minutes, he inserted the disk into the stereo and hit Play.

"Hello! I'm Dr. Robert Benson. If you are listening to this, then I am in eternal peace. The only one who could have answered all the questions to open this safe was my son, Joe. I assume I am talking to you, Joe. Please listen carefully, son. Inside this safe is a signed prescription by me, a licensed physician, authorizing the vial of medication to be injected into you and all my remaining family members. Show the formula documents to one of the medical professionals listed on the sheet in the safe so it can be replicated for others. They are all friends and colleagues.

"The medication cures cancer. It will also preserve your life in the event of a deadly chemical war or a plague. The medication will mutate in your bloodstream and remain with you throughout your lifetime, protecting you and preventing your body from hosting any cancer cells. Cancer, of course, is not a contagious disease. Joe, remember that for it to work, your mind has to be pure. It cannot be abused by the intake of toxins. You must also be without stress. All the medicine in the world cannot cure or protect you if your mind does not have peace eternal!"

Joe laid down on a couch in the study then positioned himself so his forehead was hanging off the edge and facing up. This increased blood flow to his brain. Joe closed his eyes and remembered his father. Tears flowed down toward his forehead, then dripped off and fell to the floor.

"Joe," the recording continued, "if Lumbra is still with the family, please ask her to administer this medicine. I know that she was studying nursing along with archaeology. I love you, Joe, my son. I wish I had said that to you more while I was living. Remember, Joe, whenever you think about God, then God is with you at that moment. Always do good things, son. And take care of your sister, my beautiful angel daughter. God bless all my family members with the bliss of eternal peace!" Dr. Benson's message concluded.

Joe allowed his father's message to enter deep into his subconscious mind. "I know what Father is trying to tell me," he said aloud. "Cancer is a disease of the spirit. If someone is not healthy and peaceful, it could come back even after they have been cured."

Joe shared the recording with his family. They decided it was indeed a good idea for Lumbra to administer the medication. She had just received her registered nurse's license. She had always worried about what would happen if she were on an archeological expedition in the middle of nowhere and there was a medical emergency. Who would take care of her team, and at a low cost? Dr. Benson convinced Lumbra that being self-reliant was best, so she had decided to become a nurse as well as an archaeologist. Lumbra smiled as she thought about the great Dr. Benson, who had helped her in so many ways.

She administered the medication to Joe, Rose, Napoleon, General Benson, herself, and even Herbie. He had volunteered with enthusiasm, chanting, "Herbie! Herbie! Herbie!"

After Lumbra gave Herbie the shot, he said, "Herbie live forever!"

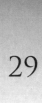

29

Joe was chosen to represent the United States at an Olympic fencing competition. This was partly a result of Napoleon's connections in the fencing world, and partly due to General Benson's Water Mason affiliations and political connections. But of course, Joe qualified in first place because of his extraordinary fencing abilities. He loved walking around the house proudly in his official Olympic uniform. He had become a master swordsman and fencing expert thanks to his two teachers, Sensei Musashi and Napoleon.

One night at dinner, as the competition was drawing near, Joe said enthusiastically, "My family, I would be extremely happy and honored if all of you"—he looked at each of them—"Grandfather, Rose, Lumbra, and Napoleon would accompany me to the Olympics in England. It would comfort me and help put me in a Zen mindset if I knew that my family was there cheering me on."

Everyone got up from the dinner table and said, "We would be honored to be with you!" Napoleon and the general shook Joe's hand while Lumbra and Rose hugged and kissed him. Herbie swooped in from some hiding place, landed on Joe's shoulder, and asked, "Herbie go Olympics? Herbie go Olympics?"

Joe laughed. "Yes, Herbie, you're family too. Herbie go Olympics!" He picked Herbie up and cradled him. He squeezed him gently and then kissed his head. Herbie kissed Joe all over the face with his parrot tongue.

Napoleon set various French dishes down on the table and announced, "Dinner is served! Bon appétit!" He made his famous popping noise. *Pop!* Everyone sat down, said grace, and began to eat. They washed the meal down with freshly squeezed fruit juice. As always, there was a pot of coffee on the table for anyone who wished to have a cup of joe.

—☷—

Joe, accompanied by his family, traveled to England to compete at the Olympic Games. He easily made it to the final round of competition. The United States vice president had walked into the American's Olympic fencing team room. He observed they were about to say a few words in prayer.

"Actions speak louder than words of faith. I want a gold medal, and I want to see blood!" He had proclaimed aloud to the entire fencing team.

Joe calmly looks at the vice president. "If you have no faith in your words, then your actions will not have success!" The vice president clinched his fists and walked out of the fencing room as he glared at everyone. The room was now quiet as Joe led a few words of prayer to the Father. The American fencing team, inspired by Joe, begins the final qualifying matches. After Joe's last qualifying match, he took a break by sitting on the floor with both palms in his lap. He placed his right palm on top of his left palm, with his thumb tips touching. Joe closed his eyes and began peaceful breathing to relax his mind. Thinking of nothing and meditating helped him generate chi.

Far away in Japan, Sensei Musashi was preparing to watch his pupil on TV when suddenly there was a major earthquake. Musashi calmed down all his family members and said, "Accept that the earth must move, just as the wind blows and the sun shines. Life and death are one. Accept whatever will come to pass so that you have eternal peace as the true Japanese do. This is the way!"

Musashi turned on the television. "Joe!" he said aloud to the screen. "Show the world that you are a true samurai, and show the world the way before the world is no more. You will prove that honor still exists for those who seek it by accepting that life and death are one. Knowing this liberates you to actually enjoy life!"

The Musashi family sat down to watch on their two-hundred-inch television with surround sound. One of the family members brought Mr. Musashi tea to help him relax while he watched his favorite student. The TV announcer stated that Joe would duel with an English athlete, Sir Ivan, for the gold medal. Both had already defeated many competitors from other countries.

The camera showed Joe's family seated in the audience, rooting for him. The United States vice president, alias Blood Heart, sat in a secured box seat nearby. His eyes gleamed with fire as he looked at General Benson. He still feels classmate General Benson is too patriotic and was responsible for his problems he had at West Point many years ago. General Benson did not politically cover for him; consequently, Blood Heart was removed from West Point for acts of plagiarism. General Benson believes integrity is an important value, for that reason he had never entered into politics.

"Gold medal, Joe!" General Benson shouted. "Honor your country! If you win the gold medal, you'll definitely be going to West Point!"

"That's my brother!" Rose yelled. "You can do it, Joe!"

"Be careful!" Lumbra added.

"And have fun!" said Napoleon. "But be serious too! You have the tools. You can do it!"

Even Herbie joined in by crying, "Joooooe!"

Joe finished meditating. His internal battery was charged up with plenty of chi. He chomped patiently on sunflower seeds as he got ready for the match, which was due to begin in just two minutes.

The two young athletes walked onto the mat gracefully, like two young lions. They held deadly lethal dueling epées in their hands. They made eye contact then saluted each other with their swords. The duel was about to begin. They each smiled to the audience. A new Olympic rule allowed the athletes in the finals to choose whether or not to wear any chest protectors or masks. Sir Ivan voted not to, and Joe concurred. They had opted not to, so this could possibly be a duel to the death, thus giving more pride for the country they represented. Young women screamed ecstatically from the audience—they were attracted to Joe's extremely handsome face and chiseled physique. There was also something magnetic in his eyes. Some young men saw a prototype hero in Joe. They all waved and screamed for his attention.

"Joe!"

And the King of England said, "Unbelievable!" He was in attendance with his bride. He had to restrain a young woman from the royal family, for she was very infatuated with Joe's looks.

However, many Englishmen locals shouted, "Poppy cock! Sir Ivan will bloody kill that American!"

"Let's see how he does in combat!" England's king said proudly. "Looks are not everything."

The Olympic referee announced the rules. "Due to this is a fencing match duel, fencers are allowed to move left or right on the strip, as well as forward and backward. Three rounds of three minutes each. The first fencer to total fifteen cuts or stabs against his opponent wins the gold medal! The winning fencer also has the option to take his opponent's life. However, he also has the option to spare his opponent's life. Consider whether your countrymen will view your choice as positive or negative before you decide!"

Joe and Sir Ivan moved into the starting position. The professional referee shouted, "En garde! Ready! Fence!"

The bout began. The audience bit their nails with their eyes wide open. People watching on TV at home stopped answering phone calls or doorbells. Everyone throughout the world was watching these Olympic fencers' every beautiful, artistic move. And both fencers footwork looked as if it were a smooth ballet dance. Joe did a false advance to lure or see what response Sir Ivan would do. However, Sir Ivan just stayed in the en garde position.

Joe instantly thought, *This is going to be a chess game against a great opponent.*

Sir Ivan thought to himself, *Yes keep moving, American, so I can get your bloody timing down!*

Sir Ivan quickly moved forward with a non-telegraphic ballestra, which is a hopping step from the back foot leaving the ground while simultaneously the front foot is in a midair lunge forward. Ivan straightens his weapon arm for an extension, attempting to spear Joe. But Joe instinctively and extremely fast retreated out of range.

The art of Olympic fencing is a beautiful ancient art to behold! thought the king of England.

The Olympic fencers moved forward, backward, left and right of their opponent, looking for an opening to attack! People felt they were watching a Robin Hood or gladiator movie, only better because it was real, and the possibility of death loomed. The fencers moved their swords circle 4, which moves the blade in a small counterclockwise motion and then circle 6, which moves their blades in a small clockwise motion as they begin to feel each other out to attack.

Sir Ivan, testing Joe in the danger zone, extended his sword out as he pointed it at Joe, attempting to draw blood. But Joe swatted it away with a powerful parry out of the center line, then riposte a deep feint attack to Sir Ivan's nose. Sir Ivan's eyes lit up like the moon, but Joe smiled as he backed away.

"Not just yet!" Joe shouted. He used an ancient *Art of War* strategy to psychologically wear down the opponent. It's as if Joe was playing a game of cat and mouse. Joe has various feint techniques or fake attacks, which seems like attacks, but not all of his feints are the same so he can fool his opponent. Joe realized it's useless to feint cut the experienced Sir Ivan from an inch too far away. The right move from the wrong distance is no move at all. Sir Ivan started to bounce up and down with his experienced springy legs as he attempted to use deception for an attack. Sir Ivan's blade flexed up and down with every bounce to create a blade-deception attack.

Joe, however, closed his eyes and went into a samurai Zen sleeping trance to speed up his reaction time. When Joe was in this Zen trance, not even a bullet could touch him. As Sir Ivan spotted Joe's eyes close, he salivated, thinking of a possible kill strike! Then he did a direct attack on Joe, which is straight to the target without diversion. But Joe had a great samurai sensei and fencing maestro. He slowly opened up his eyes to hear his heart slowly beating.

As Joe's blade smoothly circle parried to intercept Sir Ivan's sword, the American quickly riposte a counter attack, but Sir Ivan did a spanking parry in defense. Then Sir Ivan safely retreated back into the on-guard position. Joe remembered one of his penetrating tactics to gain an extra touching reach on Ivan. Joe moved forward. He advanced with his weapon arm out for an extension and smiled with confidence.

Sir Ivan looked into Joe's eyes as he retreated, wondering what Joe was up to. Suddenly, Joe—with his sword extended—put all his weight on his front foot, leaning forward while his rear foot was off the ground; he kept extraordinary athletic balance, and reached out piercing the blades tip inside Sir Ivan's ribs.

"Auh!" Sir Ivan painfully screamed in disbelief. Joe did not do a kill strike yet for he feels somewhat reluctant to end someone's life. However, Sir Ivan is an experienced gladiator—a master swordsman. Sir Ivan, with warrior tolerance, spotted Joe plant his feet and captured his timing for a split second. Sir Ivan slashed his razor sharp sword at Joe's upper torso, cutting his skin to profusely spit out blood. The crowd is going ecstatic with the blood and violence.

As the Olympic fencing battle for gold medal continues, there are more cuts and more stabs. The Olympic referee keeps tract of the score of cuts points for Sir Ivan and stab points for Joe as the first round ends. The cleaning crew cleans up the blood on the floor, while the medical team administers aid to Joe and Sir Ivan.

The second round is about to begin as the Olympic fencers square off again. Joe and Sir Ivan get into the en garde position, face each other completely still, yet feeling each other's desire to become champion of the world and win the Olympic gold medal.

The referee shouts, "En garde! Ready! Fence!"

Meanwhile back in Japan, Sensei Musashi says softly to the television screen, "Focus, Joe. You know the way, you are a samurai!" His mouth was dry with excitement, so he drained his cup of tea. "Bring me more tea! More tea!"

A family member brought him a tray that held a family heirloom—priceless porcelain teapot with one small empty teacup. Instead of pouring himself a cup of tea, Musashi grabbed the teapot full of tea and started drinking straight from it. The entire Musashi family looked at him in astonishment.

"What?" he asked. "Can't an old man just drink some tea?" He went nonchalantly back to drinking from the teapot and ignored the onlookers! This was an Olympic fencing—gold medal match!

Suddenly, Sensei Musashi's sixth sense kicked in. He felt something big was about to happen around him! But he couldn't put his finger on what? He continued to watch the fencing duel, tense but joyful. He saw Joe as a son to carry on his legacy.

At that moment, Sir Ivan did a fleche, a running kind of step combined, with a low-line thrust of his sword. But Joe defensively contacted Ivan's blade with a beat 7 and followed with a horizontal slash, cutting Ivan's thighs and producing shock in his nervous system. Sir Ivan begins to sweat profusely. Joe did another attack—a graceful feint with his sword at Sir Ivan's left shoulder—threatening Sir Ivan, which drew a reaction. Sir Ivan attempted to powerfully parry Joe's sword but missed. *Whiff!*

Joe used lightning speed and changed his sword's direction, for a painful deep cut slash across Sir Ivan's chest. Then Joe quickly flicked Ivan's blood off his blade to the ground, which is a samurai *chiburi*.

The vice president drooled like a vampire when he saw the blood and continued sadistically smiling at General Benson.

Joe sensed Ivan's rage. He had established that Ivan had a high tolerance for pain, which is a mark of a champion. Sir Ivan did a quick lunge with a straight thrust, attempting to spear Joe's heart. But Joe quickly flicked his sword with his wrist for a beat, a crisp strike of his blade, against Ivan's. Then he made a possible riposte strike to touch center mass of Sir Ivan's body. Unbelievably, experienced Sir Ivan did an impossible oppositional parry to defend his life, capturing Joe's blade in an engagement. While both blades were maintaining contact—connected in an engagement—Sir Ivan looked for a possible opening to disengage his sword for an attack. However, Joe was careful to keep his blade engaged with Ivan's so he could feel his opponent's energy. As Joe controlled the energy of the center line and slid his squeaking sword, Sir Ivan moved forward and walked right into the sword's point. He was speared deep in the shoulder.

"Argh!" Ivan screamed in pain.

The vice president began sweating profusely. He grabbed a towel to wipe it off with and started pacing.

Most of the men in the audience shouted for Ivan, who had home court advantage. "Ivan! Ivan! Ivan!"

But most of the women from various locations in the stands shouted for Joe.

"Kiss me, Joe!"

"Marry me, Joe!" Eventually, a few women tossed out nice aromatic smelling flowers at the American Olympic fencer.

Sir Ivan, bleeding from his shoulder, heard the women. He seethed with envy and swung his sword wildly at Joe. He did not care if he loped Joe's head off. Joe moved away, untouched with fluid mobile feet as if he floated away like a butterfly. However, Sir Ivan was a champion. He was very agile and did not tire very easily. With his fencing mobility, he did a running kind of step with his sword arm fully extended—a fleche to possibly score on Joe's center mass chest.

Joe miraculously curved his body backward as Ivan's sword thrust past over his chest. Sir Ivan's eyes were in shock as he missed scoring on Joe. Suddenly, both fencers' swords engaged again. The swords connected like magnets as they looked into each other's eyes, looking into the souls for a weakness. Patiently they felt for a proper time to disengage swords, or for the first to disconnect their sword. This was sword play at its finest. Neither fencer trusting the other, but the experienced Sir Ivan suddenly took a small step forward. It was a beguiled move, a dirty move, as he kicked Joe slightly above his lead foot ankle to create shock to the body system.

"Uh!" Joe said. Somehow the English referee did not see the illegal cheap shot, for something unbelievably got into his eyes at that moment. Joe also struggle slightly for balance. Sir Ivan seized the opportunity and disengaged his sword while he attempted to thrust it deep into Joe's upper torso heart area for a possible deadly pierce-kill strike! But Joe regained rhythm as he fluidly sidestepped to his left to simultaneously parry away Sir Ivan's deadly sharp sword.

Clank!

As the referee finally cleared up his eyes, he moved around the fencers like a professional while a local shouted at him, "Get ye some glasses, you bloody old fool!"

Suddenly, someone throws a fruit from the stands at Joe's head, but he ducked as it flew by—hitting the referee in his nose. *Splat!*

The referee quickly grabbed his nose, bleeding in pain, he looked up into the stands. But the people shrug their shoulders and nodded their heads no, as if no one saw who threw the fruit?

The proud Englishman and Olympic referee proclaimed, "I'll find out who broke my bloody nose!"

At that moment, the experienced Sir Ivan felt a window of opportunity. "You're nervous, I see it!" he shouted at Joe. "You're a bloody American fool!"

Joe felt slighted and thought to himself, *A fool? Why is Ivan bad-mouthing me?*

Ivan instantly took advantage of Joe's slight pause for thinking! And he scored a slashing-cut-point across Joe's powerful abdominals. Behind Joe, a piece of wood mysteriously popped up from the ground, tripping Joe. He fell back hard on the floor, a knock-down blow which is heavily penalized, evening the match according to the English referee, who now wears a heavy bandage over his broken nose. Joe wondered how Sir Ivan had managed to trick him.

The vice president flung his smelly, sweaty towel at General Benson, but it fell short. General Benson just laughed and shook his head in disbelief.

Joe got up from the ground quickly in an attempt to parry Ivan, who was lunging at him with a lethal death strike. The unexpected happened. Joe suddenly remembered Napoleon's story about why he had lost at the Olympics.

He also remembered Sensei Musashi saying, "Do not let someone control your emotions. Only you can control yourself and your emotions. This is the way of the samurai. To win against any adversary, you must feel honor within you. Connect with your own honor, then act!"

Joe twisted his body as Sir Ivan's blade grazed across it by the width of a human's hair. The champion Sir Ivan was not done. He spun his sword horizontally around his body for a medieval technique. He tried to cut Joe in half, but Joe did a boxers bob and weave, ducking underneath Ivan's sword. As Ivan's sword missed Joe, it sliced off one of the referee's fingers. *Flop!* His heavy fat finger hit the ground.

"Ahr!" The Olympic referee screamed. That's the end of the second round. Unfortunately, the medical team could not find the referee's sliced off finger as they chased away a dog, so they just bandaged up the referee's hand.

"Bo Bo! Get back here!" the old Englishman shouted to his English bulldog. It returned to the owner, chomping a piece of meat.

They were now into the third and final round, after the medical team patched them up again, where a death blow would immediately win Olympic gold. The referee had a grapefruit-size bandage over his broken nose, white bandage wrapping around the stump on his hand where the finger once was. Yet, the referee with medication in his bloodline, moved liked an Olympic professional.

The king of England commandingly looks at Sir Ivan. He sees and feels the pressure and decides enough is enough!

I'm the champion! I'll win this for the king! Sir Ivan says to himself. He swings downward on Joe's head, attempting to split it in half. But Joe steps slightly to his left with samurai skills, while his sword goes up high to receive Ivan's sword with an *uke nagashi*. Then Joe releases Ivan's blade underneath as it falls to the floor, disarming Ivan, then quickly cuts Ivan across the chest with a short slash forward.

"Uhrrr! You bloody bastard!" Ivan screams. The referee calls time! Joe takes a drink of alkaline water to replenish liquids then waves to his family that he's fine. Sir Ivan, an experienced swords master, quickly regained his composure and retrieves his deadly sharp sword. The medical team cleans up both Olympic fencers and informs the referee that both are ready for battle.

The referee shouts, "En garde! Ready! Fence!"

Sir Ivan, not wasting any time, reached from his vest pocket and threw some black pepper at Joe's eyes and nose. Joe immediately started to sneeze while his vision blurred. Joe desperately positioned his sword in front to protect his centerline from any thrust attacks, but he did not know were his opponent was. Sir Ivan took a quick battle breath, focused his deadly sharp sword, then attempted to plunge a death blow in Joe's heart.

Joe, a true Samurai with grit naturalness of a warrior, went into a deep Zen trance and connected to his sixth sense. He said to himself, "Don't think. Just feel!"

Sir Ivan launched his line of attack at an angle, to penetrate Joe's centerline defense. But Joe, laying his life on the line, knew the art of dying and was ready for whatever may come. Joe—with economy of motion—fluidly used a powerful doublé. It disarmed Sir Ivan and broke his sword in half, cutting him in the face while it spun through the air. Sir Ivan stumbled in pain and fell to one knee.

Joe, sweating and bleeding, pointed his sword a few inches from Ivan's chest, ready to strike the death blow. The crowd went silent. Sir Ivan was frightfully sweating and bleeding in his face; blood dripped profusely and fell to the floor. Sir Ivan was helpless like a lamb; his eyes were wide open in shock. He could taste the sweet-and-sour blood on his tongue.

The sadistic vice president was devilishly crying with delight!

Joe smiled modestly at his humbled opponent. He chose the option to spare Ivan's life. He knew he already had enough points to win, so he graciously offered Ivan a hand up. Sir Ivan, still bleeding from his face wounds, accepted Joe's hand. Sir Ivan looked a bit bewildered when he saw his sword on the floor, in pieces. Joe the American had won the gold medal!

Joe's family jumped for joy, while the men in the audience—composed of mostly Englishmen—fell silent.

The vice president alias Blood Heart threw his beverage on the ground angrily; it splashed on people sitting next to him. He stormed out and shouted, "I hate peace!"

Once the few seconds of silence passed, the young women become ecstatic again, screaming and crying for the handsome young hero. Some of the young men also felt like talking to Joe or shaking his hand. Many fans attempted, but only a few of them broke through the security barrier and showered Joe with determined kisses, passionate hugs, handshakes, or pats on his back. Joe felt humbled and jubilant to display an act of peace.

Back at the White House, the president of the United States was watching on a big-screen TV with his cabinet. When he saw Joe's merciful act, he stood up and said, "Joe showed the world that peace eternal is good! Invite Joe to the White House. I want to have a beer with him!"

"It's an honor to be in this great country, and it's an honor to compete in these great Olympic Games. Please, ladies and gentlemen, take a seat and show honor! Thank you!" Joe said, trying to free himself from the group of excited fans.

"Yes, yes, honor!" the women said.

"Honor? You bloody fool, you just beat Sir Ivan. No one ever beats Sir Ivan!" the men said. They all eventually went back to their seats, but kept leering at Joe.

The English fencing team was obviously disappointed and envious. "Look at that bloody American fancy-pants," they grumbled. "He showed us up!"

Back in Japan, Sensei Musashi jumped into the air. This had been the finest fencing duel he had ever seen. He dropped the priceless beautiful porcelain teapot; it broke into seven celestial pieces. He had felt satisfied in his heart with peace eternal and celebrated with his family.

All of a sudden he clutched his heart, looked up to the sky as if he could see someone there, and said, "Yes, Gabriel. I have always believed!"

Mr. Musashi fell to the floor, dead of a heart attack. It all happened right in front of his family. A few minutes later a huge tsunami, an aftereffect of the earthquake, hit Japan. It swallowed the remaining members of the Musashi family.

—⚔—

One of the English fencing team members informed his teammates that Joe was the son of Olivia Benson, the famous, extraordinary English ballerina. The English team had convinced themselves that they only lost to Joe because he had a proper English bloodline. Sir Ivan was unaware of Joe's English heritage, of course, but he was a man of honor so he shook Joe's hand again to congratulate him on his victory. Joe knew that a samurai's sword was linked to his soul. A samurai could take life or give life. Joe had chosen to spare Sir Ivan's life.

Ivan returned to the English fencing team's area to drink some water and wipe the sweat and blood off his face. There, he learned who Joe's mother was.

"Yes!" he shouted. "I knew there was something special about him!"

The medical team cleaned up all the courageous Olympic fencing warriors and prepared them for the medal ceremony. The king and queen of England and the queen's younger sister, Charlotte, came down to present the medals personally. The king introduced himself, his queen, and his sister-in-law, Charlotte.

The king smiled as he placed the gold medal around Joe's neck. "You beat the English fencing champion, who everyone said was unbeatable. Legends I heard as a child said that only a benevolent knight of honor could beat an unbeatable warrior. If you have any personal requests, please let me know. I would like to invite you to the castle for a small ceremony. Please bring your family and your girlfriend or wife."

Joe smiled. "I have no girlfriend or wife, but I do have some family here with me. Thank you. It would be an honor. I will come."

The queen shook Joe's hand, smiled, and then joined her husband. Charlotte stayed behind and smiled coyly at Joe. He lifted her fingertips gently to his mouth, bowed, and kissed them. Charlotte blushed then hurried to catch up with her sister.

The king placed the Olympic silver medal around Sir Ivan's neck next.

"Forgive me, sire!" Ivan said.

"When our citizens learn lessons, it improves our country and makes it stronger. I watched how you humbled yourself. You showed our country to be an honorable one by the way you congratulated Joe on his victory. Sir Ivan, that was your choice, as it was the American's choice to spare your life!"

Sir Ivan smiled in appreciation. "Our country is blessed to have such a wise young king." He dropped to one knee to show respect.

Finally, the king placed the Olympic bronze medal around the neck of a French athlete, and as a leader, said to him, "Thank you for competing. You showed the world that France has men and women of honor!"

"Merci, monsieur le roi!" the French swords-man replied.

The king returned to his seat next to the queen and Charlotte. The ceremony concluded when "The Star-Spangled Banner" was played. General Benson, Rose, Lumbra, and Napoleon were all extremely ecstatic. They shouted their proud approval.

Herbie jumped back and forth among the family's shoulders, squawking with pride. "Gold medal Joe! Gold medal Joe!"

Word spread quickly around the Olympic stadium that Joe was the son of the late Lady Olivia, the famous

English ballerina. Before long, the news also reached the ears of the king himself.

As the US anthem finished, Joe looked up at the king and said loudly, "Your Highness, I would also like to honor my mother, the late Lady Olivia Benson, by having her country's anthem played, too, please."

The king nodded in approval, granting Joe's request. As "God Save the Queen" began to play, tears streamed down Joe's face.

—⚡—

The Benson family had plans to tour some of England's historical sites. So the next day, Joe arranged to visit the king alone. Only Herbie joined him, insisting, "Herbie go with Joe! Herbie go with Joe!"

Joe entered the royal palace with Herbie on his left shoulder. He showed his invitation to the palace guards. A few phone calls were made, and he was patted down to check for weapons. They even looked under Herbie's feathers. Joe and Herbie were escorted to see the king.

The king greeted Joe with a firm handshake, which Joe returned. They clearly had mutual respect for each other.

In the reception room, a large open window looked out to a view of the beautiful royal gardens. Herbie craned his neck to look at Joe.

"Yes, Herbie. Ha, ha, of course! By all means, go enjoy yourself in the gardens!" Joe said.

"Later, Joe!" Herbie said on his way out the window.

The king invited Joe to sit. Displaying extreme confidence, Joe athletically glided across the floor as graceful as a lion on the hunt for prey. He took a seat next to the king. They talked about battles. The queen and her sister stopped in for some quick refreshments, and then left since the king had requested a private meeting. The men discussed life and the loss of parents, which they both had in common. A bond of friendship quickly formed between them.

Two swords in a porcelain box bearing the royal crest were brought out to the young king. The king offered Joe a sword and invited him to a duel. The young king was determined to test Joe's sword fighting skills for himself. They went at it for a little while before Joe knocked the king's sword from his hands.

"You're too good for me, Joe! Will you give me a few lessons?"

"It would be an honor to teach you, Your Highness!"

He admired the balance and feel of the king's sword as he twirled it around in his hand. He gave the king a few lessons in swordsmanship. While they were taking a break, Charlotte gracefully entered the room again.

A servant, who happened to be a former British naval officer, strode in and offered them tea or coffee. Charlotte was just gazing happily at him, so Joe took the lead and said, "I'll take a cup of joe, please."

"A…cup of joe?" Charlotte asked, unfamiliar with the American slang. Luckily, the servant had understood what he meant.

"A cup of coffee each for the gentleman and lady it is," he said and bowed on his way out.

The chemistry between Joe and Charlotte was immediate. She studied his muscular hands while they drank coffee and made conversation.

At one point, Herbie flew back in and said, "She's a keeper, Joe!" Joe and Charlotte just smiled.

"Look at Joe," the king said to his queen. "He is smooth! It looks like he's having fun with your sister."

"I hope he comes around more. He is a young man of honor, and he could protect you, my husband," the queen said.

"Yes, his fighting skills are out of this world. It's almost as if he were a knight from heaven. I believe it's time, my queen, to bestow a knighthood," said the king.

He walked straight up to Joe and said boldly, "Joe, this royal ceremony is for you. Please listen to everything I have to say before you answer. I want to make you a knight and a peer of the realm so that your skills can help defeat evil, not just in my kingdom, but throughout the world. I want you as one of my private knights. You would help to keep England strong, just like in the old days. The world does not know I have been gathering knights around me. I can only protect my knights' identities if they are anonymous. That way, they are safe to go about their missions of chivalry. Of course, you would not have to live here at the palace. You would only need to respond when duty called. A few of my knights even live in other countries, not all good men can come from one area. I will honor any decision you make."

"Honor...yes, it would be an honor to accept your offer. I will be knighted, just like Robin Hood was knighted! I want to help good defeat evil."

The handsome young king smiled. "The way, Joe, you know it! You will be called Sir Joe, Knight of Honor."

Joe called his family to request that they come to the ceremony. They arrived just as it was about to begin. He introduced them to the young king and queen.

"Grandfather, you've been to Europe many times," Joe said. "But I hope you had a great time touring the sites today."

"I never get tired of seeing England," the general said. "All the people here are friendly to foreigners, and there is so much history. The food is excellent, too, because there are so many good chefs!"

"Oui, Europe has good chefs," Napoleon agreed. "But they cannot compare to the best chef, c'est moi!"

"Tranquilo, mi amor," Lumbra whispered quickly. "Calm down, my love."

The small ceremony finally began. It was a very traditional proceeding. The king made a short speech about why Joe had been selected for knighthood. He listed the values and characteristics required of a knight: courage, chivalry, tolerance, initiative, manners, amiability, listening skills, observational skills, leadership, intelligence, concentration, self-control, confidence, swordsmanship, athleticism, and faith in God.

With Herbie on his left shoulder, Joe got down on one knee before the king and said, "Yes, I accept knighthood with honor!"

The king touched Joe on both shoulders with the flat side of his sword's blade, careful not to harm Herbie. "Joe, you were selected to be the Knight of

Honor. With my power as king, I dub thee Sir Joe, Knight of Honor."

"Herbie knight?" the bird asked.

"Herbie is now a squire," the king said with a smile. "And when Sir Joe witnesses Herbie demonstrate bravery and valor in battle, then he shall make Herbie a knight." The king lifted his sword high. "Arise, Sir Joe, Knight of Honor!"

Joe stood up proudly. The king presented him with a sword inscribed *Sir Joe, Knight of Honor*.

Joe held it high in the air. "I am the Knight of Honor and while I live, I will honor this world. I will use knowledge from Sensei to show the world the way!"

Everyone clapped and cheered for Sir Joe. Immediately after the ceremony, a royal celebration was held. A buffet table was covered with huge trays of excellent food and drink.

The king proclaimed loudly, "Everyone enjoy the night. We are here to honor England's new Knight of Honor, Sir Joe Benson!"

Everyone clapped, and Rose began to play a grand piano in the center of the room and sing. Herbie found his groove and danced back and forth on the piano's lid. Rose and Herbie made a good team. A few musicians accompanied them in a modern dance song. Joe's male hormones came alive as he danced charismatically with Charlotte. The king held his loving queen as they danced up a storm as well. General Benson talked with a British general about his various military experiences and exchanged war stories. Napoleon was deep in conversation with the royal chef until Lumbra pulled him away and onto the dance floor.

30

The entire Benson family returned home from England. They sat together in the living room eating peanuts, sipping on cups of joe, and watching television. The news was all about the earthquakes that had happened around the world and the subsequent tsunamis that hit Puerto Rico, Cuba, Australia, the Philippines, Japan, Taiwan, and Hawaii very hard. Joe had tried to call Sensei Musashi as soon as he heard, but he couldn't get through. Joe confided his concern about Sensei to his grandfather.

"Please don't worry," the general said. "Let's try to enjoy the John Wayne movie that is going to be on when this emergency news flash is over. The news always seems to be about something bad happening around town or in the world these days. There, it's finally finished! Listen, Joe, don't worry about your teacher. I remember a John Wayne movie where this little Japanese guy threw John Wayne all over the place effortlessly. This was right after John Wayne beat up a huge Japanese man who was the little samurai's friend. So you see, the samurai way is unstoppable. You will see your Sensei Musashi again, as God is my witness."

The movie began. It was called *The Searchers*.

"This is based on a book by Alan Le May," the general said. "The book and the movie are both good. I recommend reading the book later. It will make you appreciate the movie even more. Remember, readers are leaders!"

As General Benson munched some peanuts, Joe said, "I understand there is a new Western movie out called *True Grit* with Jeff Bridges."

"Yes. I've already ordered it on Blu-ray. I can't wait to see it. Jeff Bridges is one of my favorite actors. He was great in the *King Kong* remake. Man, how afraid he was of that big gorilla until he stole his woman! Life is about overcoming adversities."

Rose rolled her eyes. "Oh, Grandfather, please! Give me a break. Wasn't that movie about a giant ape? Like some ugly big monster would really capture a nice young woman."

"Let's just watch the movie," said the general.

"I like the courage that the heroes show in Western movies," Joe said. "Unfortunately, not everyone has courage like that."

The general rubbed his chin. "Courage is important, but so is the ability to concentrate. What I like about this movie is how John Wayne stays completely focused on his goal of finding his niece while he overcomes temporary adversities."

"I like the sword the cavalry soldier, John Wayne's son, has in the movie," Joe said.

"I hope John Wayne rescues his niece from that bad Chief Scar!" Rose exclaimed.

General Benson laughed. "Remember, Rose, this is just a movie. Someone has to be the bad guy, and it's not going to be John Wayne. After all, he's the star of the movie. As John Wayne himself would say, 'That'll be the day!'"

"You know, Rose," the general continued, "you should know something about Native Americans. I have a good friend named Chief Owl. We go fishing once or twice a year. He's very intelligent and has a master's degree in world history. He told me that when we fish together, we're calming spirits who wronged each another in the past. Our ancestors."

"Each race and culture has its own type of beauty," Rose said. "My English mother sacrificed living in her own culture to live here because of father."

"So did Napoleon," Joe chimed in. "And Sensei Musashi who lives in the United States half of the year."

"Don't forget Lumbra!" the general added.

Another news flash interrupted the movie. "Israel has elected a new leader called Mr. Natas. He has made no secret of his plan to use Israel's military power to influence other countries to conform to one world order, or to try and extend his own role as leader. Mr. Natas is a smooth talker who speaks many languages fluently."

Someone knocked at the family room door. Joe took the opportunity to practice using his sixth sense and guess who it might be. "It sounds like Lumbra."

General Benson laughed. "Who else would it be? Lumbra, please come in."

Lumbra entered, wearing a wedding dress that shows off her full figure. "How did you know it was me? Como supiste?"

Napoleon came in behind her in a nice tuxedo. "Bonjour, family!" he said with a pop. Lumbra had tears in her eyes.

"Casamos! We got married! We didn't really plan it. We just went down to the courthouse and did it. We have come to say good-bye."

Napoleon shrugged. "Spontaneity. It must be the French in me."

The Bensons all rose to congratulate them. Everyone hugged and kissed.

"I will miss you, Lumbra and Napoleon," Joe said. "You both were like older siblings to me."

"When you won the gold medal in fencing, Joe, it lifted a weight of disappointment about my own failing off my shoulders," Napoleon said. "I felt so defeated when I had to settle for the silver. But you won the gold, and you are my student, yes? This means that I must be a great fencing teacher. You gave me back my honor!" Napoleon slapped his mouth hard with his hand to give Joe a very loud pop of gratitude. Joe laughed. Napoleon had been making that sound ever since he was a child, but Joe still enjoyed watching and hearing him do it.

Lumbra gave Joe and Rose a hug and a kiss each. "I am only leaving this beautiful house, not your lives. But I have to pursue my dream of finishing my father's work. Now that I'm an archaeologist and an RN, Napoleon and I will launch an expedition to the Island of Patmos and use my father's map to find his former dig site.

"Joe, your father was a great man! His cancer treatment has been released to the Salk Institute and to a doctor friend in Israel. Your decision to release his research will help mankind live longer. You know that a few years before your father found the cure for cancer, he also found the cures for AIDS, Parkinson's, arthritis, and Alzheimer's. As a biologist and physician, Dr.

Robert Benson certainly made his mark in the world. Now I will make my mark in the world, too. I will discover what is hidden in Patmos by completing my father's last archaeological expedition!"

Napoleon and Joe went into the garden to gather some fresh vegetables and fruits thereafter, while General Benson went to get a few gallons of natural water from the well. Napoleon prepared a meal for them all, and they had a great last supper together. Afterward, Lumbra hugged and kissed everybody good-bye, including Herbie. She seemed to be at a loss for words.

The Bensons and Herbie stood at the front door and waved good-bye to Lumbra and Napoleon as they drove away.

Joe said, "Au revoir, Napoleon, my great fencing teacher!"

With his beautiful wife on his arm, Napoleon waved back. "Good-bye to you too, Joe!"

31

It turned out that the earthquakes and tsunamis were only the beginning. The world economy also began to crumble when snow fell on regions where it never had before, destroying crops and raising food prices to enormous highs. An enormous volcano erupted, and then another, darkening the skies with ash. This lured out many insects, which began to bite animals and humans and devour crops to survive. Huge numbers of livestock died. Volcanic ash contaminated many drinking water supplies and covered huge swaths of grass cows and other livestock needed for grazing. The food chain all over the world was in crisis. In the major cities, citizens formed long lines in the streets just to get one cup of government-issued drinking water. Earthquakes and tsunamis continued to happen in both the Pacific and Atlantic Oceans, causing fish to die and depleting the world's food supply even more.

Around the world, people began to turn away from God. Several countries, including the United States, even passed laws prohibiting people from wearing a cross or any religious symbol in public. Violators were fined heavily, and if they were unable to pay they were jailed or made to work for free at government camps. While Dr. Benson's antidote kept people from dying because cancer or AIDS, they began to drop dead in the streets due to a lack of food and clean drinking water.

The smooth-talking leader of Israel, Mr. Natas, bought television airtime to broadcast a message to the world. He wanted to convince the largest countries to form a ten-nation world order and appoint him as its supreme leader. The countries eventually agreed. People living in those ten nations received food and drinking water, however, only if they displayed a mark on their right hand or forehead that proved they were in allegiance with Mr. Natas.

—☰—

One day, Joe received an e-mail invitation for an all-expenses-paid trip to visit the new capital of the Ten-Nation League. His sixth sense told him not to go; he feared it was a trap.

"Yeah, right," he said aloud. "Nothing is for free!" He deleted the e-mail and shut down his computer.

That same day, General Benson received a call from the president of the United States.

"Arnold," he said, "I want you to accompany me on a trip to the Middle East to attend a Ten-Nation League meeting being held by Supreme Leader Natas to brainstorm how to stimulate the world's food supply and economy. Bring your grandson with you. Mr. Natas says he wants to meet Joe, the Olympic fencing champion and gold medalist."

The five-star general had always trusted his gut instincts. He wondered why the president would ask specifically about Joe. He decided to leave Joe at home, but knew he himself could not refuse to attend. "Yes, sir. I promise I will go, Mr. President."

The general said good-bye to Joe and Rose and, like any loving grandfather, asked them each for a huge, memorable hug and kiss.

"Don't worry," he assured them. "I'll be back before you know it. But duty calls."

"Trust your instincts, Grandfather, and call us when you get there," Joe said. General Benson immediately turned around to face Joe and said, "Do you remember the fishing and camping trips we took, grandson?"

"Yes, Grandfather. I remember the sun rises from the east and sets in the west. I remember the moon rises from the east and sets in the west. I remember to follow the North Star at night—not to get lost. I remember how to eat roots, bark, and how to find an underground pocket of natural water to drink. I remember how to snare a fish out of water, and a wild turkey on land. But what I remember most was how you read the words of God from the scriptures while you wore that big tanned Stetson hat!" Joe replied.

At that moment, General Benson took off his tanned Stetson hat and placed it on Joe's head. Joe smiled with pride. "Looks good on you, grandson. *Sehr gut!* (very good!) Yes, it's time. This old soldier of many battles needs to go out to pasture. Remember to trust your gut instincts, Joe. Remember, your grandfather loves you both!" General Benson said.

"We'll miss you," Rose added. "The world is a dangerous place. Please don't leave us like Mother and Father did."

"Now, now, Rose. You're one of God's good angels. You will see me again, I promise. Joe, you take care of her, okay?" He did not tell Joe that Mr. Natas had asked him to bring Joe on the trip.

Joe waved good-bye as General Benson slowly exited the house, taking a last look around. Herbie flew down, seemingly from out of nowhere, onto Joe's shoulder and nibbled his ear.

"I will take care of you, Rose," Joe promised. "And I believe Grandfather. We will see him again."

"I take care Rose! I take care Rose!" Herbie squawked.

General Benson got into his armored jeep and drove away to meet the president on Air Force One.

—⁂—

Joe received a call on his royal cell phone; all knights of England were issued one.

"Europe is in a state of crisis about leader Natas," the king said. "I will likely call on you for your services soon, my loyal Knight of Honor. In case I cannot, then I want you to use your initiative and go to the part of the world that needs you most. You are the Knight of Honor, Sir Joe, and currently one of my healthiest knights. A deadly virus is spreading throughout the world and killing innocent men, women, and children. The royal families, including myself, for all had taken the vaccine left by your great father, Dr. Benson, to our personal physician. The vaccine does cure this new plague, but terrible leader Natas has made sure that its mass reproduction is slow."

"Your Highness, why is this all happening? Why have I been blessed not to be infected by this plague?"

"Sir Joe, things happen for a reason. You will see in time why you have been spared."

"The world is blessed to have such a wise young king. Thank you for your advice on the way of life."

"All your brother knights have been activated around the world. At least, the healthy ones have. One final note, Sir Joe. My sister-in-law, Charlotte, is on her way to see your lovely sister perform in Beverly Hills. Please take care of Charlotte and send her back as quickly as possible."

"I understand, sire. I will send Charlotte back immediately after the concert."

32

Word arrived that the president of the United States had been assassinated while at the Ten-Nation League meeting. General Benson had also been taken hostage. Nuclear reactors in various parts of the world had also started leaking radiation due to all the seismic activity. The devoted power plant workers were diligently trying to make repairs and put their hearts into their work, but the reactors were nearly impossible to stabilize.

Despite all this, Rose's piano concert was still scheduled to take place at an arena in downtown Beverly Hills. Joe and Rose were not yet aware that their grandfather was a hostage. Joe, Rose, and Herbie traveled to the concert in Dr. Benson's aging but still fast Mercedes-Benz SLS AMG supercar. Due to a rise in crime from desperate people, Joe used the arena's armed valet parking. With Herbie on his left shoulder, Joe held Rose's hand as he escorted her up the steps to the concert hall. As they approached, they could see that people had fallen dead on the surrounding streets from the plague.

"So much death," Joe said. "Our father worked hard all his life to find cures for diseases. A cure for this plague exists thanks to him, but not everyone is getting it. It's as if the devil wants humans to suffer." Joe had felt since the world seems to be ending. Maybe its best to let the person you love know how you feel.

"Joe, our family was saved by Father's vaccine," Rose reminded him. "We have to be grateful and remember that things happen for a reason."

Joe nodded in agreement while he and Herbie shared some trail mix; it was a combination of flax seeds, sesame seeds, sunflower seeds, and pumpkin seeds. Before the concert began, the Benson family provided the audience with free food, drinks, and concentrated sea kelp pills to help flush their thyroids of any radiation.

Rose stepped up to the microphone and said, "My late father, Dr. Robert Benson, wanted us to think positive. We, his children, are here to encourage you to do that tonight." She and Joe waved. Their warm smiles resembled their mother's—they both had an entertainer's pleasant demeanor.

Charlotte arrived with her royal bodyguard. She was wearing an exquisitely beautiful dress. Charlotte and Rose hugged and kissed like ladies. Joe lovingly hugged Charlotte and took her by surprise by kissing her passionately.

"I've missed you," Joe confessed.

"Herbie kiss?" the bird asked, and she obliged. "Wow!" he squawked.

"Check yourself! I'm watching you, Herbie," Joe said. "Remember, I'm the knight, you're just a squire." Everybody laughed.

The concert was about to begin. Herbie said, "My cue! So long, Joe." He took his customary perch on the piano.

"I will now play something to inspire us all to be honorable!" Rose said. She began to play the grand piano. "Let It Be" was her first song.

Charlotte leaned over to Joe. "I have taken your father's vaccine. I thank you from the bottom of my heart for making it available to my family!" She kissed him deeply.

Joe enjoyed sitting with her in the front row and watching Rose sing and play musical masterpieces. Herbie felt the rhythm and got into his groove, moving from side to side across the piano.

A wealthy young man sitting in the crowd with his parents was emotionally infatuated and said, "Look at her, Mom and Dad! Her voice and face are so beautiful!"

"I believe our son is in love," the mother said.

"Indeed he is. Maybe we could arrange something, dear?" the father concurred.

At that moment, Joe became aware that the handsome young man was smiling deeply at Rose. He clapped his hands thunderously after each song she played. Joe couldn't help but notice that he was wearing a Water Mason ring on his finger, just like his grandfather's.

Suddenly, Joe felt his cell phone vibrate in his pocket. He prayed it was news from his grandfather. But it was Lumbra.

"Joe, por favor, can you please come to the Island of Patmos?" she pleaded.

"Why?" Joe asked.

"I discovered something. It's a petrified-wood carving of Jesus Christ with his arms extended in front of him. He's holding a sword with both hands. The sword is engraved with markings I don't understand. I know you are an expert on swords. I need you. Can you please come here to help me decipher these?"

"I guess I could, but I don't want to leave Rose alone," Joe said.

"Ask her to come with you si ella tiene tiempo (if her busy schedule allows)."

"Lumbra, esta bien! Say hi to Napoleon for me."

The concert continued. Joe snuggled up next to Charlotte and kissed her hand. It seemed to the two of them as if they were alone in the huge auditorium. Joe knew the moment has come. He pulled out a small box and opened it. Inside, a priceless blue diamond ring sat on a cushion.

"Life is not forever," he began. "The world seems to be ending, so there doesn't seem to be any sense in wasting time telling you how I feel. I want to be engaged to the woman I love. Will you marry me?"

"Yes, Sir Joe!" Charlotte exclaimed, beginning to cry. "I love you with all my heart! Everything I have is yours, my love!"

Joe hugged and kissed his new fiancée. He wanted to fill his mind with powerful memories of this moment in time, but his instincts told him there was danger ahead.

He looked up to the sky and said quietly, "Thank you, God, for this moment."

When the concert came to a close, Rose could see that a few people had dropped dead in the audience from the plague. She stood up and said, "People, please don't be afraid of these hard times. Together we can overcome all adversities. Please have faith in God!"

One of the people in the audience shouted, "Arrest that woman! Call the police! She mentioned God in public! That's against the law!"

A security guard nearby shrugged. "Sorry, I didn't hear what she said. Too bad, sir…er, madam."

He turned away and helped himself to the free food and drinks. Times were hard.

Rose walked up to talk to her brother and Charlotte. "You both look so happy, but I can see that Charlotte's been crying. What's happened?"

Charlotte showed her the beautiful diamond ring. Rose hugged and kissed her future sister-in-law.

Herbie said, "Honor, Joe! You showed honor!"

"Joe, the whole orchestra and I have been invited to give a concert for Mr. Natas and the League. Please may I go?" Rose asked.

"Well, I guess you can go. You'll be safe with all your musician friends, and Grandfather is there…somewhere. I am going on a trip, too, to see Lumbra and Napoleon in Patmos. Rose, you must promise to meet up with Grandfather if you can and to call me when you do."

"I promise, Joe! I love you!"

With hugs and kisses all around, they said good-bye.

—∞—

Across the world, General Benson was being beaten heavily by his captors. When they had finished torturing him, they placed him on a huge dirty wooden cross. He panicked when he realized that they apparently intended to crucify him. He struggled but was overpowered by six huge men. They used hammers to drive rusty large nails through the general's palms and his bound feet. It felt like great thorns were tearing his flesh and ripping at his nerves as they went through his body. Blood and tears flowed out of him profusely, and the brave war veteran screamed in enormous pain. Once he was hanging on the cross, a foul-smelling Mr. Natas appeared to interrogate him.

"I wanted you to bring your grandson here. You disappointed me!"

"What do you want with him?" the general groaned.

"Joe is the chosen one! Your window of opportunity is closing, General. Your life depends on your ability to convince Joe to come here."

With courage and honor, the general said, "Burn in hell!" Then he started to pray. "I believe in God, the Father Almighty, creator of heaven and earth. I believe in Jesus Christ, who sits at the right hand of the Father. Jesus shall come to judge the living and the dead!"

While General Benson prayed, Mr. Natas ran his long, claw-like fingernails cutting skin down his chest, drawing blood. Then he began ripping big pieces of the general's flesh away to inflict the most pain possible.

At that moment, in extreme agony and with tears in his eyes, General Benson looked up to the sky and said, "Yes, Gabriel. I've always believed!" And then he was no more.

33

J oe escorted his fiancée, Charlotte, to the airport with her bodyguard.

He kissed her good-bye and said, "Remember me! Things happen for a reason. And remember that I'll love you always."

She looked into Joe's handsome face and said, "I will always love you, Sir Joe. Remember, you are the Knight of Honor. My heart will always be with you, my love!"

She boarded her plane to England, and Joe and Herbie boarded a plane for Patmos.

When their plane arrived, Joe made sure he had his royal sword by his left side and at the ready. Lumbra and Napoleon were at the airport to greet him.

"What is that amazing smell?" Joe asked. "Is there something good to eat out here in the middle of nowhere? I'm famished!"

"Herbie famished! Herbie famished!" the parrot agreed.

Napoleon laughed. "It just so happens I brought something that I whipped up for you. Here, have some. I've missed both of you." He handed Joe a nylon bag full of fine food and then made his customary popping noise. "Bon appétit!" *Pop!*

"Just like old times," Joe said.

"Old good times, Joe," Herbie echoed.

Joe laughed. "I guess he means I'm no chef, Napoleon."

Lumbra took them all to the archaeological site. She showed Joe her assortment of archaeological tools. She had various trowels and shovels for digging, a Panasonic CF-30 Toughbook laptop for recording data from an electronic soil probe, a gradiometer to measure subtle alterations in earth's magnetic field caused by buried objects, a Trimble 3600 Total Station surveying tool that her father had used on his last expedition, a Suunto Navigator Compass, metal detectors, a portable X-ray machine, and a Geoscan RM15-D resistance meter. These had helped her to pinpoint the artifact of Jesus Christ.

While Joe continued to eat, Lumbra explained, "It took an enormous amount of digging to find, but that's the main part of an archaeologist's job. It was also the part I enjoyed most as a little girl." She showed him the wooden figure. "Look at the sword that Jesus is holding. Can you read the markings?"

Joe wiped his mouth, took a drink of water, and then examined the carving. "It's the sword of the Archangel Michael. It says, 'He who has honor is like unto God.'"

Suddenly, the clouds overhead parted and beams of light shone down directly on the carving.

The figure of Jesus Christ came to life and spoke. "I am the beginning and the end. Don't be afraid."

Lumbra and Napoleon fell to their knees in fear, but not Joe. Truly the day of the Lord had come like a thief in the night, just as the Bible promised. No one on earth knew He was here but Joe, Napoleon, and Lumbra.

Joe extended his hand and said, "I feel your goodness. I am not afraid."

Jesus shook hands with him. Jesus' hand felt to Joe like friendly, moving water.

As Jesus floated above the ground, he said, "I cannot touch the earth's ground anymore, for it is tainted by sin. Neither can any angels from heaven touch this soil. God, who created man in his image, has placed the earth's salvation in the hands of man. Now only man can save man. You, Joe, are the chosen one. You can save the earth. It is up to you to accept God's mission for you."

"Lord Jesus, I accept God's mission, whatever it may be."

"Take this holy sword of Michael the Archangel. God will be with you! A powerful, evil dragon will try to control or kill you, but do not be afraid."

At these words, Joe suddenly felt adrenaline pump into his body. Drawing on his faith, experience, confidence, honor, and courage, he said to Jesus, "What must I do with this beautiful sword? I do still have my Knight of Honor sword as well." He gazed in fascination at the beauty and weight of Michael the archangel's holy sword.

"Give me your royal sword," Jesus said. "I will give it back after you complete your holy mission to restore man's honor to God! You must go to where I was among the living. You must go to Jerusalem. You need to save your sister, Rose, from the evil that has placed sin in this world. Napoleon and Lumbra will be safe here on Patmos, for I am here now."

Napoleon now felt that he had achieved peace eternal. "Adieu, Joe," he said. Lumbra was on her knees next to him, praying and looking at Jesus.

"What about my grandfather?" Joe asked.

Jesus gave him a comforting smile. "God is with you, Joe. You will see your grandfather again someday, as the Father has promised."

Joe took the holy sword and turned to leave the island. Herbie rode on his shoulders as they walked briskly to board a travel ship. "Herbie help Joe!" the bird said valiantly. As they moved quickly, Joe smiled and gave his brave friend some crackers to eat. Finally they arrived. There it was. A sailing ship that Christopher Columbus would be proud of. A mast, hull, and sail with a blonde Greek skipper at the helm. Joe walked up the ship ramp and saw a big-nosed conductor taking fairs but also turning passengers away. They attempted to board the local travel sailing ship, which embarked for Jerusalem, but halfway up the ramp they were stopped by the man.

"Turn around parrot man! No American dollars accepted here." the conductor said. Joe smiled and handed him a pouch of gold American coins. The big conductor with a huge nose smiled curiously and bit a few gold pieces. "These will do fine, nice American. You and your parrot may board ship!"

"That's right! Big nose. Awk!" Herbie shouts.

The conductor looks back at Joe. "Did you say something, American?"

"Have a good day, nice conductor," Joe says.

The conductor smiles and waves his big welcome aboard hands at Joe. However, somewhere in the near distance, lurked a tall, skeletal, evil-faced, darkly clothed, shadowy figure who's horribly upset that Joe boarded the ship. As they were out to sea, the muscular forearms of the skipper steered the helm, while Joe and Herbie helped with the sail. The cool, whistling sea air and salty ocean water hit Joe in the face and eyes.

It's a beautiful feeling to sail in the open sea, Joe thought.

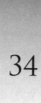

34

Joe arrived in Jerusalem and immediately headed for the League headquarters. He and Herbie ate some trail mix on the way to keep their energy up. When they came to the Wailing Wall, a good feeling flooded over Joe. He sat down with his legs crossed in the lotus position to pray and meditate.

"God, give me strength. Even if I should lose my life, please save my sister, Rose. I love you, God. Amen!"

"Amen!" Herbie said.

Joe positioned his palms on his lap with his thumbs touching, slowly closed his eyes, and went into a deep Zen meditation. He cleared his mind of troubled thoughts to rejuvenate his chi. As he slowly came out of his meditative state, he could hear a pipe organ playing music.

"Rose! Rose!" Herbie cried.

Joe believed the bird. Ever since Rose was a little girl, Herbie had sat next to her when she played; Joe knew he could identify her playing even from a distance.

Joe trotted toward the music. It led him to the Dome of the Rock. He entered and saw Islamic inscriptions on the walls with some minor Christian influence from time of King David. He looked at Koranic scriptures all around him.

Joe read, "Just like mankind became confused with different languages at the Tower of Babel, mankind has also been confused with different religions. There is only one God!" Joe paused. "Who could have the power to confuse all of mankind?"

Suddenly, he heard a loud, evil laugh. Joe quickly unsheathed his razor-sharp sword with both hands and placed it slightly above his head, in a horizontal position. This was an aggressive samurai fighting stance called the *jodan kasumi kamae*. This stance had been taught to Joe by Sensei Musashi to battle a dragon. Joe continued to move forward—toward the source of the music—toward the source of the devilish laugh. As he circled the famous rock inside the Dome, he saw what looked like a hoof mark on the holy rock's surface.

Interesting! Joe thought. He continued advancing forward—toward an unknown evil sound!

At the rear of the Rock of the Dome was an exit that led to an outside courtyard. He went out and found himself in a huge arena that held a beautiful outdoor stage. It reminded him of San Diego's Balboa Park arena. A man-made lake was next to the stage.

There was a foul-smelling, fermenting dead body odor in the air. Joe's sixth sense told him something evil was lurking nearby. Suddenly, a frighteningly huge man dressed in black armor and carrying a long, double-edged sword appeared on the stage. Then Joe saw Rose. She was shackled to a chair next to a huge outdoor pipe organ and crying.

Joe bravely walked toward them, adrenaline pumping. He was ready to perform his mission. "Let my sister go. Now!"

"Do you know who I am?" the man in black armor cried.

"I recognize you from television. You're world leader Natas. But I follow a higher leader!" Joe smoothly changed from his samurai fighting stance into his Olympic fencing en garde ready position.

The huge man laughed with no remorse. "I will let your sister go if you give me your sword and follow me as your leader!"

Rose, with tears in her eyes, began playing a beautiful wordless song called "En Aranjuez con Tu Amor" on the huge outdoor pipe organ keys.

Joe's sixth sense felt he was being lured into a trap, and he felt beguiled. So he said, "Natas, you're lying! I feel it! You have no authority over me, so lay down your sword and ask for forgiveness from God!"

Fire ferociously shot from Natas's eyes! "I am Satan! Fool!" he cried as supreme evil came across his face to transform into a demonic horror.

The ground shook as Satan swung his heavy, deadly sharp two-edged sword at Joe. But Joe, a little frightened by Satan's demonic look, athletically eluded him with good footwork mobility. Brave Herbie flew toward Satan, flapping his wings in his eyes, pecking his eyes with his beak and clawing with his claws deep across Satan's face. Then Satan ferociously struck the bird with mighty swing of his sword.

Pop!

Blood flowed out of Herbie's belly, but he had given Joe the opportunity he needed. Joe used both hands for power to slash his blade using a *hidari gyaku kesa* deep across Satan's own belly. Satan shrieked in pain and made a horrible, inhuman, evil sound. The sound of the dragon—the ancient serpent—the beast! Joe quickly flicked his sword downward, tossing Satan's foul-smelling blood to the ground.

The severely wounded Herbie landed on the pipe organ next to Rose. Herbie loved his Benson family. As if unfazed by his injuries, Herbie did his best to dance his usual left-to-right way, while Rose pumped hard on the pipe organ.

"Joe! Joe! Joe!" he cheered as the pianist Rose played masterfully.

The stage cracked open a few feet as gases and sounds from hell exited. Then Satan's demonic horror face morphed into its original visage as handsome Lucifer, who had once been the grand cherubim in heaven. Lucifer was the conductor of celestial music beautiful in every way until sin was found in his envious heart, and he was cast out of heaven with a third of all angels he beguiled.

A fierce battle ensued between Joe and Lucifer/Satan as Rose continued to strum organ keys and pump organ pedals to the song "En Aranjuez con Tu Amor." Rose's brilliant classical music playing inspired Joe's heart of a champion, and he could feel his chi aligning. Unfortunately, Satan remembered, too, when he was still Lucifer, listening to celestial music played in heaven with the Lord.

Joe lunged a straight thrust with the point of his sword, but Lucifer/Satan did a stop thrust stopping Joe's attacking blade. Joe, with quick tempo, swung his sword with two hands—a *kirioroshi*—attempting to lop off the dragon's head! But Lucifer/Satan, a divine master swordsman, intercepted Joe's deadly sword attack.

Both swords engaged hard, which cause a spark of fire to explode in the air. Immediately, Joe tried several deceptive feints with his blade to lure Lucifer/Satan closer so that he could strike him using the Archangel Michael's divine sword. But his enemy would not be fooled easily, for he alone was the master of beguile.

Lucifer/Satan slowly extended his sword out, as did Joe to engage, connecting both swords. Joe had done such *tsukikage* swordplay drilling many years with his Sensei Musashi. Lucifer/Satan, however, anciently conniving, slide his sword in slightly, cutting Joe on his face to spill out blood. Tears came out of Joe's eyes; it flowed across his face, into his cuts, and he felt the pain. Yet, Joe kept his blade engaged with tolerance and raised it up high, lifting Lucifer/Satan's sword.

Both swords were in an engagement above their heads. Joe used sensitivity and felt for an opening, then disengaged his sword for a dropping cut or *kiriotoshi* aimed at Lucifer/Satan's forehead to use the *moni-*

uchi—the last nine inches of the blade's tip. In the danger zone, Lucifer/Satan quickly moved; but Joe's blade cut off a piece of the beasts left shoulder, and it fell to the ground like a piece of raw meat. *Flop!*

Lucifer/Satan growled in pain again! He went ballistic on Joe with no remorse and focused his evil desire on him. Joe used the water strategy, which is to respond like an echo to your opponent, and leapt over Lucifer/Satan with his extraordinary athletic ability while swinging his sword for a possible hit. But Lucifer/Satan swung back his heavy double-edged sword, attempting to cut Joe in half! Both swords clanged loudly, making another huge spark that started a small fire on the stage.

Joe, now in a perfect fencing on-guard stance, did a fleche for a possible attack. Lucifer/Satan laughed and did something Joe never saw before. Lucifer/Satan devilishly dropped to the floor then wiggled his belly and legs on the floor to slither away, like a snake, and mysteriously disappear.

Unbelievable! Joe thought. No human, including Joe himself, could do that mobility move to escape an attack. Unbeknown to Joe, Lucifer/Satan slashed deep across Joe's knees, which spilled out large amounts of blood.

"Auh! Ouh!" Joe cried out in immense pain. He stumbled backward away with footwork to safely recover.

Lucifer/Satan drew an evil smile, knowing Joe can mortally die, and advanced on Joe, looking for a death strike. Lucifer/Satan violently attacked Joe; their swords clanked high! Clanked low! Clanked left! And clanked right! Then Lucifer/Satan did a sword thrust aimed at Joe's human heart. But Joe quickly intercepted the sword with a circle parry in defense.

Joe, tiring from loss of blood, used his weaponless hand with hardened martial artist knuckles to punch like a boulder rock into Lucifer/Satan's face. *Crack!* Lucifer/Satan, the ancient dragon was dazed. But he blindly continued to thrust his sword toward Joe, attempting to spear Joe's human flesh anywhere. However, it seems Joe was trained since childhood for this battle, as he eludes all spearing strikes. Joe is a true samurai, fearless and evasive with chivalry of an Olympic gold medalist fencer.

Somehow, due to Joe's powerful swordplay, Lucifer/Satan dropped his sword. Nevertheless, he viciously grabbed Joe by his shirt, pulling him in, trying to bite him like an evil animal! But Joe struggled away—tearing his shirt wide open and exposing his muscular chest, arms, and ribbed abdominals.

"Man should never have been the image of the Father!" Lucifer/Satan devilishly screams. Then he angrily grabbed for Joe's holy sword. Unable to take it away from him, he wrapped his smelly, fungus-filled arms around Joe and pulled him into a clinch.

Joe's eyes watered from the foul, decaying odor of the devil. He struggled but was unable to free himself. Lucifer/Satan, salivating at the thrill of this moment, opened up his foul mouth filled with toxic germs and deadly viruses. The devil's smelly, greenish-yellowish shark teeth bit violently deep into Joe's shoulder.

"Auh!" Joe cried. Joe immediately felt warm blood that profusely sprung up from an artery, while they both struggled for possession of the powerful sword. Joe's muscles strained and flexed while he bled in enormous pain. Joe tried to overpower the handsome Lucifer/Satan using brute force, but the devil was too strong for him.

Lucifer/Satan's handsome and beautiful features was actually a mirage. His face morphed back into its evil-looking version, the ancient serpent, the dragon, the devil. His foul-smelling mouth revealed large, sharp, fungus-ridden teeth. The vision of horrendous Satan, with its sulfuric odor, charged Joe like a bull with horns!

Suddenly, a lesson from Sensei Musashi flashed into Joe's mind. With complete concentration, Joe focused on sensing Satan's energy to use body connection and to use *ukenagashi* receive and flow. Joe felt a few of his ribs crack as he absorbed Satan's rushing charge, as if he was struck by a rushing rhino. Joe wrapped his hands and arms around Satan and felt nauseous as he connected with Satan's evil energy.

Joe, who is badly injured, quickly desired to redirect this dark evil force and said, "God! In the name of Jesus. Please help me!" Joe instantly felt a temporary rejuvenated energy. He somehow flipped the heavy Satan over his shoulders and slammed him so hard to the ground, which caused an earthquake felt around the world.

Satan, like a cat with nine lives, landed near his powerful sword, which he had owned since when he was in God's righteous light of celestial heaven. But now, he is in the dark. Satan grabbed his now demonic sword and attacked Joe with a renewed intent to kill.

Another lesson from Sensei Musashi flashed into Joe's mind—the Bushido—literally "the way of the warrior," which he had learned thoroughly. Bushido stressed the samurai moral code of frugality, loyalty, martial arts mastery, and honor unto death.

Laying his life on the line with true warrior liberation, Joe held firmly the sword from heaven and inhaled deeply, breathing in one of God's most precious gifts—oxygen. He put himself into a Zen trance and focused on gathering as much cosmic chi as he could. He summoned from his body of man, in the image of God, all of his energy for a lethal thrust and then buried the powerful Archangel Michael's holy sword deep into Satan's chest. The celestial sword's thrusting blow was fatal.

Satan screamed in pain. Thunder hit the ground as voices from hell shouted the beast's name. Satan leaned on a pillar—helpless, lifeless, and could not move. With the holy sword of Michael still buried in Satan's chest, Joe pushed the evil beast off the stage and into the lake. The entire pool instantly burst into flame.

Joe was in tremendous pain. Bleeding and exhausted, he ran slowly with warrior swagger and unshackled Rose.

As Rose tearfully hugged Joe, Herbie the Parrot croaked his last words to his best friend.

"Joe! Joe!" he softly said and fell over, dead, on the keyboard. Joe held his pet parrot and cried with immense tears.

—⟶⟵—

Peace and honor began to reign over the earth immediately. Two large school buses arrived at the

Dome of the Rock just as the battle ended. The first bus contained both Palestinian Arabs and Israeli Jews, who were chatting like they were old friends, or brothers and sisters. The second bus contained Rose's orchestra friends and the group's conductor.

Rose wiped blood off Joe with a wet towel as the conductors bus approached.

"Rose, are you coming back home with us to California?" the conductor asked. "We are on our way to the airport. It would be an honor if you would join us."

"You go home, Rose. I'll catch the next flight," Joe said tearfully. "I want to bury Herbie here in the Holy Land."

"Of course, Joe. Say good-bye to your friend Herbie in your own way." She kissed Joe and got on the bus.

Joe, still bleeding from his shoulder, walked and mysteriously—a huge bleeding snake—slithered out of the lake. Walked until he reached the foot of the Mount of Olives. He entered the garden of Gethsemane. "I guess this is the place my sixth sense has guided me to. I will bury you here, my friend, Herbie!"

With tears in his eyes, Joe kissed his dead parrot. He laid him on the ground and began to dig a hole. Some of Joe's blood dripped into it as he worked. He began to feel faint. Joe felt as if his life's last blood flowed out from him. Joe thought he might suddenly fall asleep here with his friend Herbie. Joe almost fell into the hole as he dug and began to pray.

"Father! Lord God! If it's my time to die and go into a deep sleep, then thank you, Lord, for my time in life as a man!" Joe proclaimed.

Joe, slowly fainting, suddenly saw Jesus. He was wearing glowing white robes and coming toward him. He noticed that his feet were now softly touching the earth with every smooth stride.

"Man's honor has been restored on earth!" Jesus softly said. Jesus then placed both of his hands on Joe's severely injured shoulder. The wound stopped bleeding and then healed miraculously. "It's not you're time to die yet, Joe. Wake up, Joe! I will show you the Father's light. Come with me, I will show what you have been searching for, your peace eternal."

Since childhood, Joe had searched for peace eternal. He had desired for his mind, heart, and soul to have a state of calm and quiet with infinite duration.

Joe extremely exhausted. With tears in his eyes, he gently picked up dead Herbie. Jesus escorted them up to heaven. As Joe observed a brilliant orb of light, the pearly gates opened to them. Jesus calmly touched

Herbie, who was cradled in Joe's hands, and he immediately came back to life.

"Awk!" Herbie said.

"Herbie!" Joe shouted in joy.

"Herbie sleep deep, Joe. Irk! Joe, Herbie feel great!" Herbie says.

Joe laughed. "Herbie, you clown! And my best friend. You were brave and showed valor in battle. I guess that makes you a knight, Herbie! I dub you Sir Herbie!"

The parrot flapped his wings. "Wow! Herbie knight! Whatever Joe want!" He kissed Joe with his beak and his little black parrot tongue and then flew off into heaven.

Joe could not believe what he saw next. There before him, he was greeted by his father, mother, grandfather, grandmother, and Sensei Musashi.

The angels Gabriel and Raphael, along with the powerful Archangel Michael, all shook Joe's hand and said, "Heaven has regained its honor!"

High above them all, was what looked like a throne made of beautiful blue sapphire stones, and upon it sat someone who appeared to be a man with the image of man. From the waist up, he seemed to be all glowing bronze, dazzling like a fire. From his waist down, he seemed to be entirely flame. On top his head was a glowing halo, like a bright rainbow of many colors, while all around him shined an orb of light. It was the glory of Lord God who sat on his throne in heaven with Jesus the Son of God on his right side.

Then God said to Joe, "The H in heaven stands for Honor. Kneel thee down before me!"

Joe knelt down before God. "Yes, Lord God!"

"Joe, you will always be a man. I created man in my own image. I love you! I grant you eternal life and the power to travel between heaven and earth on holy missions of honor. I dub you, Joe, the Archangel of Honor!"

Jesus, at the right hand of thy Father, placed a beautiful sword in Joe's hands. The inscription read "Joe, the Archangel of Honor."

"Lord God, there could be no greater honor. I accept!"

Joe stood and held his holy sword high. Everyone in heaven was in awe of him. Joe had found peace eternal at last. Amen.